The Story of
CIRRUS
FLUX

ALSO BY MATTHEW SKELTON

◆ ◆ ◆

ENDYMION SPRING

The Story of
CIRRUS
FLUX

MATTHEW SKELTON

BLUEFIRE

Text copyright © 2009 by Matthew Skelton
Cover art copyright © 2010 by Peter Ferguson
Map copyright © 2009 by Motco Enterprises Ltd.
Galleon and terrella illustrations copyright © 2009 by Rowan Clifford

All rights reserved. Published in the United States by Bluefire, an imprint of Random House Children's Books, a division of Random House, Inc., New York. Originally published in hardcover in Great Britain by Puffin Books, an imprint of Penguin Books Ltd, London, in 2009, and subsequently published in hardcover in the United States by Delacorte Press, an imprint of Random House Children's Books, New York, in 2010.

Bluefire and the B colophon are registered trademarks of Random House, Inc.

Visit us on the Web! randomhouse.com/kids
Educators and librarians, for a variety of teaching tools, visit us at randomhouse.com/teachers

The Library of Congress has cataloged the hardcover edition of this work as follows:
Skelton, Matthew.
The story of Cirrus Flux / Matthew Skelton. — 1st U.S. ed.   p. cm.
Summary: In 1783 London, the destiny of an orphaned boy and girl becomes intertwined as the boy, Cirrus Flux, is pursued by a sinister woman mesmerist, a tiny man with an all-seeing eye, and a skull-collecting scoundrel, all of whom believe that he possesses an orb containing a divine power.
ISBN 978-0-385-73381-6 (hc : alk. paper) — ISBN 978-0-385-90398-1 (glb : alk. paper) — ISBN 978-0-375-89532-6 (ebook)
[1. Orphans—Fiction. 2. Supernatural—Fiction. 3. Adventure and adventurers—Fiction. 4. London (England)—History—18th century—Fiction. 5. Great Britain—History—George III, 1760–1820—Fiction.] I. Title.
PZ7.S626123 Sto 2010   [Fic]—dc22   2009018987

ISBN 978-0-440-42169-6 (pbk.)

RL: 5.2
Printed in the United States of America
10 9 8 7 6 5 4 3 2 1

First Bluefire Edition 2012

For Thomas and Oliver

CONTENTS

The Story of
CIRRUS
FLUX

LONDON
18TH CENTURY

The summer of the year 1783 was an amazing and portentous one, and full of horrible phaenomena. . . .

—GILBERT WHITE
The Natural History and Antiquities of Selborne

Prologue

THE ANTARCTIC CIRCLE,
1756

The boy can hear something scratching at the sides of the boat—a restless scraping sound, as though the sea has grown claws and is seeking a way in. For countless days His Majesty's Bark the *Destiny* has been drifting through uncharted waters, crossing new latitudes, until it can go no further south, blocked by an impenetrable reef of ice and fog.

Is this it? the boy thinks. Have we finally reached the edge of the world?

He shifts uncomfortably under the blankets he has heaped on top of himself and tries to sleep, but it is so cold that the hairs in his nostrils stick together, stitched shut. For several hours his dreams have numbed him, carrying him back to London and the fields surrounding the Foundling Hospital, where only a few years ago he was making twine and weaving nets. Now he is awake on the far side of the globe, the blood slowly freezing in his veins.

The cold decides him. He must move.

The boy swings his legs over the edge of the hammock and drops to the ground. All around him men are slumped in sleep, but he takes care not to rouse them as he creeps through the cramped quarters to the stairs. For many it is their second or even their third voyage to the southern reaches of the globe and they are accustomed to such hardships. Their faces have been scoured by wind and rain, and their beards are grizzled with frost.

He finds his childhood companion, Felix Hardy, sprawled against the bulkhead door. By rights Felix ought to be above, on watch, ensuring that the boat does not run aground on the sheets of ice, but the big, burly youth has sneaked down during the night and dozed off in his heavy fearnought jacket. The boy watches him for a moment, but does not have the heart to disturb him. The ghost of rum is still warm on his friend's breath and a smile is slung across his ruddy face. Instead, the boy bunches his own jacket more securely round his narrow shoulders and climbs the wooden steps to the deck.

Outside, the light dazzles him with its brightness. The icy fog that has dogged them for weeks, ever since they rounded the tip of Cape Horn, has lifted and the sky is a pale powdery blue. Icebergs the size of cathedrals throng the sides of the boat.

The boy has never known such a desolate, beautiful place. Suddenly all of the privations he has suffered—the wretched food, the hard physical labor, the bouts of seasickness—slip away and leave him charged with excitement. Remembering the thrill he first felt when he boarded the ship at Deptford Yard, dreaming of a life of adventure, he skates from one side of the deck to the other, taking in his wondrous surroundings.

And then he senses something. A crackle in the air, a hint of sound, as though the ice itself is breathing.

All at once he can hear Mr. Whipstaff's instructions in his ear, training him in the arts of navigation: "Invisible forces be at work in this world, boys; and while we cannot always divine their origin, yet can we discern their presence. Let your mind be your compass and it will seldom steer you wrong."

In an instant, the boy is climbing the rope ladders to the top of the mast, to get a better view. The rungs are braided with ice and slip underfoot, but he is used to scaling such heights, even in stormy weather, and soon he is standing on a little platform high above the frosted deck. Up here, the air is even colder and ice fronds form on his lashes, but he brushes them away with his sleeve and stares into the distance.

Nothing. Nothing but a shining white immensity of ice and water, for as far as he can see.

He reaches into his pocket, pulls out a short brass spyglass and holds the freezing lens to his eye. His hands are so cold, the world trembles. Even so, he manages to guide the glass across the barren wastes.

And then his breath escapes in a silver cloud—a dissolving yell. For, barely visible against the horizon, something has loomed into view, a precipice far larger than any he has seen. A luminous shelf of ice, a whole continent perhaps, made, it seems, of shimmering light. It towers above the water, girding the horizon like the gateway to another world.

The boy's heart clamors inside him. He must alert the captain.

His foot is on the ratline, ready to descend, when something holds him back. A suspicion, a doubt. Bright blue flames have appeared above the mast and the air flickers with a quiet intensity. He looks up to see a scintillating stream of particles rippling overhead, passing back and forth across the sky.

The boy stands perfectly still, wondering if he has imagined it, and then glances down at the small sphere he wears on a cord round his neck—his terrella, the miniature globe on which he has been charting his travels. Some of the particles have drizzled down, surrounding it, disappearing into the metal with short, sharp flashes of light.

Slowly, as if filled with the miraculous substance, the orb begins to glow.

Startled, he drops his spyglass, which rolls across the platform and tumbles into space, hitting the deck below with a resounding thud. Instantly, the light around him dissolves and the noise is picked up by the surrounding ice, echoed and multiplied. Explosive cracks burst through the silence like cannon fire, and icebergs calve into the sea, sending huge, crashing waves spilling against the side of the boat. The boy is nearly thrown from the mast.

Almost immediately, there is a rumble from below. Cries of panic, footsteps on the stairs. Men appear on deck in disarray, seeking out the cause of the disturbance. Felix is at the belfry, clanging the bell with all his might. The ship is a hive of noise and activity.

Numb with shock, the boy clings to the mast and stares dumbly into the distance, where, to his dismay, the apparition he has seen has vanished behind a gathering wall of mist. Flecks of powdered ice drift before his eyes, blurring his vision. All that remains of the icy continent and the flames above the boat is a ghostly, lingering glow.

"Ahoy there! Boy!"

The boy looks down and sees first Mr. Whipstaff and then the captain standing below him on the deck. He opens his mouth to answer, but cannot find the voice to speak. Words fail him. Instead, he gazes down at the terrella, shimmering faintly still against his chest, and hides it deep in the folds of his coat. He knows instinctively that no one will believe him, that gleaming particles have rained down from heaven and filled his sphere with light.

Jittering more than during his first days at sea, he descends from the mast and manages to coax his shaking legs to carry him the rest of the way to the captain.

"Yes, what is it?" says Smiling Jack, with his customary frown.

The captain is a tall, gallant individual, dressed in a dark blue uniform with golden braids. He has been in a surly mood ever since the boat was blown off course and became stranded in this icy landscape.

"Speak up, boy."

"Able Seaman James Flux," whispers Mr. Whipstaff in his ear.

"Explain yourself, Flux."

James averts his eyes. "My spyglass, sir," he says, running his fingers through his wavy hair. "I dropped it from the mast. It . . . it shattered on the deck. I'm sorry, sir."

The captain glances from James to Felix, who has sheepishly approached, holding what remains of a dented spyglass in his hands. His hard emerald eyes narrow with suspicion.

"And you were the boy on watch?" he asks.

"Yes, sir," says James, unwilling to look at Felix directly in case he incriminates him.

"And pray tell me, Flux, did you see anything that warranted awakening the ship in such a manner?"

The boy doubts again that anyone will believe him; he has heard too many tales of sailors who have mistaken common gleams of light for unnatural phenomena at sea. "No, sir. There was nothing, sir. Nothing but ice and emptiness, sir."

The captain considers his verdict for a long time. "Very well," he says eventually. "At least you have found us a favorable wind. For that, I suppose, we must thank you."

The boy lifts his head. Only now does he feel the cold, cutting breeze on his cheeks.

Raising his own spyglass to his eye, the captain quickly scans the horizon, but finds nothing of interest and hands the instrument back to Mr. Whipstaff, who swiftly sheathes it in a polished tube. With a visible shudder, he turns to his second in command.

"Tell the men, Mr. Whipstaff, to raise the sails. Today, we head for New Holland. I have had enough of this accursed climate."

A cheer greets this announcement and the men are soon hoisting the sails, which flap and swell above them.

"And you, Flux," says the captain, bending down to speak to James privately. "Either you are incredibly lucky or you are damned loyal. Do I make myself clear?"

"Yes, sir."

"Now get to work. I shall be keeping my eye on you."

"Yes, sir."

A short while later, once the boat is plowing through the waves, James sneaks back to the stern and watches the icebergs recede into the distance. He is not aware, at first, of the other boy standing close beside him.

"You saw something from the mast, did you not?" says Felix, his reddish brown hair flapping behind him. Like most of the seamen, he has tied it back in a knot—although in his case, it looks more like a frayed rope than a ponytail.

James, locked in his thoughts, knows all too well that Felix will not move, will not budge from his side, until he shares his secret. There is a strong, safe silence between them. For the first time he manages a smile.

"Aye, something strange and mighty powerful, I shouldn't wonder, Felix," he says, peering into the waves that chop and churn behind the boat, erasing all memory of their passage through the water. His hands reach for the terrella beneath his jacket and he feels a strange tingling sensation pass through his fingers.

"I reckon," he says at last, "that I seen the Breath of God."

Twenty-seven Years Later

LONDON, 1783

⊰ 1 ⊱

The Gallows Tree

For as long as anyone could remember, the children had been drawn to the Gallows Tree. The black twisted oak stood on the outskirts of the city, in the corner of a field not far from the dirt road leading to the hills of Hampstead and Highgate, several miles to the north. The oak was clearly visible from the upper windows of the Foundling Hospital, and the children liked nothing more than to gather under the spell of moonlight and whisper strange stories about the tree.

"Do you see that shadow in the topmost branches?" said Jonas one night as the boys prepared for bed. "Do you know what it is?"

The boys pressed closer to the window, ghosting the glass with their breath. They nodded as a small round shape detached itself from the gloom.

"What is it, Jonas?"

"Tell us."

Jonas's voice was dark and menacing. "Why, 'tis only Aaron's head," he said. "The boy who used to sleep in *that* bed."

He pointed to a narrow cot, one of many that filled the room, causing the little boy who now owned it to cry out in fear. Barely five years old, the new boy had just left his wet nurse in the country and wasn't yet used to life in the boys' dormitory. His eyes widened in fright and large tears splotched the front of his nightshirt.

Voices circled the room.

"What happened, Jonas?"

"Go on. Pray tell."

Jonas stood for a moment in front of his captive audience and then, like the Reverend Fairweather at the start of one of his sermons, raised a forefinger in the air. "Promise not to repeat a word I say. Not to the Governor, the Reverend, nor the Lord above. Do you promise?"

"We promise, Jonas."

"We swear."

The vow passed from mouth to mouth like a secret. Even Tobias, the new boy, managed to murmur his assent.

When at last the room was quiet, Jonas spoke. A thin, pale-faced boy, he had a shock of dark hair and rings of shadow, like bruises, round his eyes.

"Aaron took it upon himself to leave the hospital," he said. "Tired of being a foundling, he was. Wanted to make his own way in the world."

His gaze settled briefly on Bottle Top, who was stretched

out on his bed, pretending not to listen, and then traveled back to the other boys, who were sitting, cross-legged, on the floor.

"But all he met was Billy Shrike."

"Billy Shrike?" asked the new boy uneasily.

"A cutthroat," one of the others whispered.

The older boys knew that Jonas was lying—Aaron had been apprenticed to a wigmaker in the city—but Jonas was the most senior boy among them, one of the few who could read and write, and his mind was a gruesome compendium of details he had scavenged from the handbills and ballad sheets visitors sometimes left behind in the stalls of the chapel. He could tell you everything, from the names of the criminals in Newgate Prison to the lives of those condemned to hang. Billy Shrike was his most fearsome creation yet: a footpad who liked to stalk the fields by night and snatch young foundlings from their beds.

Jonas swept the hair out of his eyes and leaned toward Tobias. "The felon was waiting for Aaron near Black Mary's Hole," he said, "and slit his throat with a smile . . . and a rusty knife."

The boy who had inherited Aaron's bed now streaked to the chamber pot in the corner.

Jonas's voice pursued him. "Billy put his head in the Gallows Tree to keep an eye on you, Tobias. To warn us not to let you escape. For, if you do, he'll hunt you down and—"

"Stop it! You're frightening him!"

Heads turned to find Bottle Top standing on his bed.

15

Dressed in a rumpled white nightshirt that came down to his knees, he looked like an enraged angel—except that his ankles were smeared with dirt and his wild flaxen hair shone messily in the moonlight. The air made a slight whistling noise as it passed between his teeth, which were chipped and cracked.

Jonas stepped toward him and, for a moment, the two boys glared at each other, face to face; then Jonas glanced at the new boy in the corner.

"Have we frightened you, Tobias?" he asked, with false kindness.

Tobias, crouched near the floor, looked from one boy to the other. Then he noticed the small gang slowly crowding round its leader and sniffed back his tears.

"No," he mumbled. "I'm not frightened."

"Bah!" exclaimed Bottle Top, throwing himself back on his bed and rolling over to face the wall, defeated. "The devil take you all!"

"Shhh! Someone's coming," said a voice from the opposite end of the room. Cirrus had pressed his ear closer to the door and was listening for any trace of movement. He backed away as he heard the first heavy footfall of the Governor on the stairs.

Quickly and quietly, the boys returned to their beds, while Cirrus rushed from window to window, closing the tall wooden shutters, which had been folded back to reveal the moonlit night outside. He gazed into the dark stretch of fields—at the wide expanse of grass and the huddled hills

16

beyond. Then, as he came to the last window, he noticed the Gallows Tree.

Sure enough, exactly as Jonas had said, there was a head-shaped shadow in the topmost branches; but now, standing beside the tree, there was also the unmistakable figure of a man. Cirrus could not distinguish him clearly, but the man appeared to be wearing a long black coat—just like a high-wayman—and a three-cornered hat that obscured part of his brow. His hands were cupped round a flickering flame that cast an uncertain glow on what was exposed of his face. At first, Cirrus thought it might be a lantern, but, as he watched, the flame slowly escaped from the man's fingers and rose in the air.

A key scraped in the lock.

Cirrus spun round and saw a thin wedge of light slide under the door. Immediately, he closed the wooden shutters, ran across to his bed and leapt under the covers. He lay perfectly still, hoping that his racing heart would not betray him.

Light seeped into the room and the short, stubby figure of Mr. Chalfont, the Governor, appeared. Carrying a candle, he trod up and down the dormitory, in between the rows of beds, checking on the boys, who all seemed to be sleeping peacefully, snoring at intervals.

Cirrus watched the steady advance of candlelight from under his blanket and sucked in his breath as it paused briefly above his head. He could smell the Governor's familiar aroma of pipe smoke and brandy, and was reminded of those nights, many years ago, when Mr. Chalfont had taken him aside and

17

shown him the treasures in his study. He had been just a small boy then, no older than four or five, and more interested in the private stash of ginger, which the Governor kept in a tin in his desk, than the dramatic seascapes on the walls.

"Good night, lads," said Mr. Chalfont at last, breaking into Cirrus's thoughts. "Sleep tight."

He made his way across the room, closed the door behind him and locked it.

Instantly, Cirrus was back at the window, peering outside. The figure with the lantern—if it had been a lantern—had gone and the tree was a stark silhouette, a solitary shadow by the side of the road. Cirrus quickly scanned the fields, but they were empty also. There was no sign of the mysterious stranger.

"What're you looking at?" asked a timid voice from behind him. Tobias was sitting up, watching him with moist eyes. "Is it Aaron's ghost?"

The other boys began to laugh, moaning and groaning like phantoms beneath their sheets, but Cirrus ignored them and padded over to the young boy's bed.

"It's nothing," he said gently, tucking him in. "You're safe here. Now go to sleep."

Shivering slightly, he stepped back to the window, looked out once more and then, when he was absolutely certain no one was there, returned to his bed, near the unlit fireplace in the corner. Beside him, Bottle Top was muttering something under his breath, something to do with Jonas and the Gallows Tree.

"How about you and me sneak off tomorrow and show him, eh, Cirrus?" he said.

But Cirrus wasn't listening. He was thinking of other things: of the strange figure beneath the tree and the ball of flame that had hovered momentarily in the air.

❧ 2 ❧

The Girl Behind the Curtain

The following morning Pandora was cleaning one of the upstairs windows when she noticed the two boys sneaking away from the hospital. They climbed the apple tree near the back of the garden, tied a rope to one of its overhanging branches and jumped over the surrounding wall, disappearing from view.

She watched for a while, then caught sight of her reflection imprisoned in the glass. A girl with a mutinous expression and ghastly hair—the victim of another of Mrs. Kickshaw's haircuts—stared back. Pandora glowered in response. Why did she have to look like this, dress like this and do the same tedious housekeeping, day in and day out, while the boys were free to roam outside? It wasn't fair.

She picked at the scarlet ribbon on her coarse brown uniform and found the answers lining up in her head like obedient schoolchildren: *because she was a girl; because she was a foundling; because the Governor had kindly taken her in, fed her and clothed her since the week she was born; and because she had nowhere else in the world to go . . .*

A small sigh escaped her and she watched as her doppelgänger faded in the dull glass. Then, remembering the cloth in her hand, she halfheartedly began to wipe her sigh away.

Without warning, footsteps approached and the door opened. Instinctively, Pandora backed into the folds of the heavy, half-drawn curtain and made herself invisible. She grasped the keys in her apron pocket to keep them from jangling and peered cautiously round the edge of the curtain.

Mr. Chalfont, the Governor, looked in. A portly gentleman with spools of woolly white hair, he swept his eyes round the dimly lit chamber, misjudged it to be empty and stepped aside to admit the most breathtaking person Pandora had ever seen.

A tall, graceful woman, dressed entirely in silvery blue, strode into the room. A thousand tiny frost flowers seemed to shift and shimmer across the surface of her gown as she moved, and Pandora longed to stroke the fabric, wondering whether it would sting her fingers with cold. Then, with a shock, she drew back. The woman's hair was coiled in an intricate system of loops and curls that stayed in place on their own; it was the most extraordinary thing she had ever seen.

Pandora blushed, touching her own scrub of curls, and felt the damp rag brush against her skin. There was no time now to dash the duster round the room, pretending to look busy. Nor could she politely excuse herself and leave. Mr. Chalfont would surely suspect that she had been up to no good: napping, thieving or, worse, evading her chores . . . when all she had been doing, *really*, was gazing out of the window, wishing she could be somewhere, anywhere, else.

Yet here she was. Trapped.

Fortunately, neither Mr. Chalfont nor his visitor appeared to have noticed the gently swaying curtain or the hyperventilating girl now safely concealed behind it. There was only one thing for her to do: remain hidden.

Hitching up her skirts, Pandora climbed onto the window seat behind her and knelt on the plump velvet cushions. She pressed her eye to the partition in the fabric, curious to see what would happen.

"The boy," said the woman presently, as Mr. Chalfont drew the dark wooden door shut behind them. It closed with a soft, furtive click. "Is he here?"

"Cirrus Flux?"

"You know very well the boy I mean. You received my letter, did you not?"

Mr. Chalfont moved toward the fire, though the day was neither wet nor cold—merely overcast and murky. Embers snoozed in the blackened hearth, but, brandishing a brass poker, he managed to prod them into life. Shadows began to prowl.

For a dreadful moment Pandora feared the Governor might open the curtain to let in more light, but he appeared to have other things on his mind. He kept his voice to a whisper and his motives to himself.

"I fear, dear lady, that we cannot oblige you," he said, removing a letter from his frock-coat pocket and unfolding it in his hands. "Cirrus is but a child, and not the most agreeable child at that."

His eyes drifted toward the window and Pandora cringed in her hiding place.

"I confess that, even now, he is most likely running off in the fields, causing trouble," the Governor said. "Indeed, we've had a most difficult time placing him with a master."

"Which is precisely why I have come for him now," said the woman. Her eyes narrowed. "To offer him a position. A trade."

Mr. Chalfont said nothing. Instead, he gazed into the hearth and, with a casual flick of his fingers, dropped the letter into the flames. The paper flared for a moment, then curled into a tight crimson fist.

The woman, in the meantime, stepped over to an ornate table clock.

"You do know who I am?" she remarked, removing the casing and inspecting the dial.

Mr. Chalfont inclined his head. "Of course, Mrs. Orrery."

"*Madame* Orrery," said the woman sharply. "Of the Guild of Empirical Science."

The man glanced up.

"Of the Guild of Empirical Science," she said again. "Do not think for a moment, Mr. Chalfont, that my origins—or my humble sex—should ever thwart me. I am accustomed to getting what I want."

"I was under no such illusion," the man murmured to himself, averting his face so that only Pandora, listening very carefully, could hear. He began to fumble with the ends of his lace jabot, which was knotted round his neck.

"Yet even so, Madame Orrery," he continued, "I am afraid you seek the impossible. You see, here at the Foundling Hospital, we endeavor whenever possible to apprentice young boys to masters, not mistresses, and Cirrus"—his eyes darted this time to a side door, as though he wished he, too, could escape—"Cirrus is not like other foundlings. His is a special case. His circumstances were . . . *are* . . . exceptional."

Mr. Chalfont almost choked on his choice of words, and his meager smile came slightly unraveled.

Madame Orrery studied the man closely for a moment, her powdered face pinched with suspicion. Then, pursing her lips, she calmly extended a hand, which was dominated by a large oval ring. She smoothed her fingers over its flat, moon-colored surface and somehow retrieved a miniature key from its secret compartment.

"I knew his father," she said softly, her words shivering in the air before melting into silence.

Mr. Chalfont turned pale. "I see," he said, mopping his brow with a large linen handkerchief and sinking into the arms of a waiting chair. "I do not suppose he is . . . still alive?"

Pandora did not hear the response. Like most foundlings, she longed to know where she had come from, exactly who her parents had been, and at the mention of the boy's father she had plunged her hand deep into her apron pocket, past the loop of keys, searching for the scrap of fabric she always carried with her. A patch of pink cloth with a single word embroidered across its front:

H * O * P * E

It was the only memento she possessed of her mother, a token of remembrance she had found in the Governor's study and taken without permission. She studied its gold lettering carefully, trying to draw solace from its simple message.

When at last she looked up, Mr. Chalfont was squirming in his chair. The woman had withdrawn a delicate silver object from the folds of her gown and was winding it very slowly, using her tiny key, all the while staring intently into the man's face. A pocket watch. Pandora could hear the instrument whirring and ticking, spinning time.

"Yet, even so, Madame Orrery," she heard Mr. Chalfont repeat feebly, "Cirrus is a special case. His circumstances are exceptional."

He ground to a halt, too tired—or else too dejected—to continue.

A sudden rap on the door caused them to turn round.

Madame Orrery snapped the watchcase shut and returned it to a pocket, while the Governor glanced up, bleary-eyed and confused.

"Yes, what is it?" he said as a stout, middle-aged woman looked in.

"Begging your pardon," said the woman with a curtsy, "but there's a gentleman to see you, sir. Come about a child."

"Good, good. Show him to the waiting room," said Mr. Chalfont. "I'll be with him shortly."

"As you wish, sir," said the woman, giving Madame Orrery a suspicious stare. "Are you all right, sir? You look a bit peaky."

"Yes, yes, never better," said Mr. Chalfont, blinking hard. "Just a twinge of the old gout, I'm afraid." He smiled. "Thank you, Mrs. Kickshaw. That will be all."

"Yes, sir," said Mrs. Kickshaw, with another curtsy, and closed the door.

Madame Orrery stood for a moment before the fire and then turned to face the Governor. "Are you certain there is nothing I can do to change your mind?" she said. "About the boy . . ."

Mr. Chalfont held up his hands apologetically, but shook his head.

"Very well," said Madame Orrery. "I shall not test your patience further, Mr. Chalfont. Good day."

She moved toward the door.

Mr. Chalfont appeared to have wakened from a disagreeable dream. He blustered to his feet.

"Madame Orrery," he gasped, rushing to detain her, "if you merely seek a child to assist you in your work, then why not consider one of our other foundlings?"

He crooked his arm round her ruffled sleeve and escorted her back toward the fire. "We have female children—girls, even," he said, his tongue tripping over itself in an attempt to make himself useful. "Perhaps you would be kind enough to consider one of these? We are always eager to place them."

The woman paused. "A girl?" she said, as if tasting the foreign flavor of the word.

"Very obedient girls," said Mr. Chalfont, regaining some of his composure. He leaned back on his heels and revealed the full globelike girth of his belly. "Trained in sewing and cleaning and general housekeeping," he continued, unable to stop. "Indeed, we have several in need of employment, ranging in age from ten to—"

"Enough!" said Madame Orrery.

Mr. Chalfont held his tongue and gazed down at the floor like a scolded dog, the hopeful expression on his face wavering just a little.

Madame Orrery considered him for a moment and then said, "Thank you, Mr. Chalfont. That is an agreeable suggestion."

Her eyes searched the room and a thin smile spread across her face like a ray of sunlight on a very cold day.

"If you do not mind, I think I shall take the girl hiding behind the curtain."

❧ 3 ❧

Blackguards!

"**D**on't look like no head to me," grumbled Bottle Top as he and Cirrus reached the Gallows Tree. They tore off their matching brown woolen jackets, tossed them in a heap on the ground and stared up at the dark, interlacing branches. The clump of shadow was clearly a nest of some kind: a messy bundle of sticks and twigs, patched together with mud.

"What d'you suppose built it?" wondered Cirrus aloud, scratching at the flea bites on his neck. "It's too large for a rook."

"Dunno," said Bottle Top, "but I can find out."

He peeled off his shoes and stockings, tucked his shirt into his breeches and approached the Gallows Tree. The ancient oak had once been struck by lightning, and a cindery smell still clung to it like a shadow.

"Here, tip us a hand," he said, placing a grubby foot

28

against the trunk, which was thick and knotted and scaled with green ivy—the only sign of vegetation on the long-dead tree.

Cirrus moved in beside him and helped heave his friend up to a long, sinewy branch.

"That Jonas!" said Bottle Top suddenly. "Thinks he knows everything on account of he can read. Well, I can show him a thing or two!"

With tremendous agility, he pulled himself up to the next-lowest branch and quickly squirreled across to another.

"Never mind Jonas," said Cirrus, glancing behind him. "It's Mrs. Kickshaw you ought to be worried about. She'll start ringing the bell if we're not back soon."

"Well, I for one ain't in no hurry to return," said Bottle Top, taking a moment to survey the surrounding land. "Did you see the way she was looking at me? Means to duck me in the cold bath, make no mistake."

Cirrus picked at the scabs of black bark with his fingers but said nothing. He could see dark clouds rolling in from the horizon.

"And she'll be after you, too," said Bottle Top, "with them scissors. You mark my word. First sign of a master, she'll be trying to make you look *persentable*."

Cirrus brushed a hand through his curls, which were growing back in worse waves and tufts than before. He could well remember the last time Mrs. Kickshaw had tried to trim his hair. "Just look at the state of ye!" she'd exclaimed, chasing him around the kitchen with a pair of barbaric shears. "Face of an angel with the horns of a devil! What's to become of ye, I'll never know!" He grimaced at the thought.

"Soon as we're apprenticed," continued Bottle Top, clambering further up the tree, "we'll need never take a cold bath again. There'll be plenty of hot water and fine clothes and all the food we can eat. We'll be proper gen'lemen, Cirrus, you wait and see."

Cirrus felt a warm glow of satisfaction. Unlike the other boys, who were content to be tailors and drapers in the city, he and Bottle Top were going to seek their fortunes abroad, traveling the world and sharing adventures.

"Nor will we have to listen to any more of Jonas's stories," said Bottle Top, glancing up at the nest, which was wedged in a fork between branches. "Aaron's head, my—"

Just then, several crows that had been bickering over a nearby dunghill let out a savage croak and disappeared in the direction of Black Mary's Hole, a row of thatched huts clustered round a disused well on the far side of the neighboring field. It was, Jonas told them, an area notorious for murderers and thieves.

Cirrus watched them go and then bent down to retrieve a stick that had fallen to the ground. "D'you believe what Jonas says?" he asked, trying to sound as casual as possible. "About Billy Shrike?"

A giggle snaked down from above.

"Are you afraid of him, Timid Flux?"

"No," said Cirrus, remembering the cloaked figure he had seen the night before. "But suppose—"

"S'pose nothing," said Bottle Top. "Don't believe a word Jonas says. A baseborn liar is all he is. No wonder he ain't yet been apprenticed."

Cirrus swiped his stick through the air, making it whistle.

"P'rhaps," he said, unconvinced.

He fingered the little brass medallion he wore on a string round his neck—a disk embossed with the image of a lamb, marking him out as a foundling—and turned to face the hospital. All around it new buildings were beginning to appear, eating away at the surrounding countryside, but the hospital remained as it was: a refuge for unwanted babies.

He ran his eyes along the solid brick ramparts until he spotted the row of windows directly beneath the eaves of the west wing. The boys' dormitory. *But suppose Jonas was right?* he was tempted to say. *Suppose someone like Billy Shrike had been watching them all along?*

Unable to shake off the suspicion, he moved away from the tree and stepped toward the road.

Something crunched underfoot.

He glanced down and noticed a few thin shards of bone strewn on the ground in front of him, in a patch of grass that looked as if it had been recently burned. He knelt down and examined them more closely. The brittle fragments were rolled up in brown peaty parcels—like owl pellets, he thought, only larger. Scattered among them were several pale gray feathers, so light they almost flew away when he breathed on them. They had a faint orangey tinge, like the fading glow of embers. He brushed one with his hand. The soft downy fluff disintegrated at his touch, leaving a dark residue on his skin. He sniffed his fingers. Ash.

Puzzled, he craned his neck and studied the nest more carefully. "Can you see what's inside?" he called up to Bottle Top, who was nearing the top of the tree.

"Almost!"

Bottle Top had twined his legs round a slender branch and was inching his way into the canopy. Nearly a head shorter than Cirrus, he was made for climbing and could scale almost anything—including the balusters of the great wooden staircase in the hospital, a stunt that often got him into trouble with the Governor.

As soon as he was on a level with the nest, he reached out and dipped a hand inside.

There was an almighty din from above.

Kraa-aak! Kraa-aak! Kraa-aak!

The crows were back. This time, six or seven of them, darkening the sky with their wings. They circled the top of the tree and then lunged at the small boy, cackling viciously. Bottle Top let out a squawk of surprise and dropped through the branches, trying to get away, but the crows were too fast. They surrounded him in an instant, an angry mob, and began pecking and tearing at his clothes.

"Shoo! Get away!" he screamed, thrashing at them with his arms, while they hopped from branch to branch, out of

32

reach. Then, all of a sudden, he slipped. He lost his footing and fell, tumbling all the way to the ground.

"Nutmegs!" he cursed, managing to stagger to his feet—bruised, shocked, but luckily unhurt.

Cirrus was there in a flash, fending off the crows with his stick. But it was no good. The birds were leaping all around them now, rising and falling like black flames. Wings fanned their faces. Talons brushed their hair. With a shout, the two boys grabbed their things from the base of the tree and raced across the neighboring field toward the hospital, more than a hundred yards away.

The crows followed in pursuit.

Kraa-aak! Kraa-aak! Kraa-aak! they cried, skimming low as the boys ducked and darted through the grass, holding their jackets above their heads to protect them from the diving, shrieking birds.

Then, halfway across the field, the crows suddenly stopped. They suspended their attack and fluttered back to the Gallows Tree, as though nothing had happened. They settled in the topmost branches.

Silence fell.

The boys slowed to a crawl and then dropped thankfully against the wall of the hospital.

"I've a good mind to stone them crows," said Bottle Top savagely, wiping a sleeve across his brow, which was streaked with sweat and tiny ribbons of blood where the branches had scratched him. "That bird bit me!"

"Which bird?"

"The one in the nest."

"Show me."

Cirrus grabbed his friend's wrist and swiftly uncurled his fingers. At the tip of one of them was an angry white welt.

"That weren't no crow," said Cirrus knowingly. "You been burned."

He peered back at the Gallows Tree, thinking of the feathers he had seen on the ground, and noticed a figure advancing toward them from Black Mary's Hole. A man in a dark blue coat and a tricorne hat.

"Who is he?" asked Bottle Top, who had also spotted him. "He looks just like a highwayman."

"Dunno," said Cirrus, feeling a shiver of recognition creep up his spine, "but I think he's been watching the hospital."

Neither boy moved, but they both looked on nervously as the man stopped beside the Gallows Tree and pulled a short, blunt instrument from the depths of his coat. He aimed it, gleaming, in their direction.

"He's got a pistol!" shrieked Bottle Top, scurrying behind Cirrus for protection.

The two boys backed against the wall, breathing hard, and then jumped as a loud noise clanged violently behind them. Mrs. Kickshaw was in the garden, ringing the bell.

"Cirrus! Abraham!" she called.

Bottle Top sagged with relief. "I'm off!" he gasped.

He was gone in an instant—scrambling round the corner of the hospital, past the burial plot at the back, to the place where they'd tied the old hemp rope to an overhanging

34

branch so they could clamber over the wall unaided—leaving Cirrus alone to face the swarthy gentleman at the far end of the field.

For a long, disturbing moment the man trained his sights on the boy and then, as Mrs. Kickshaw called out their names once more, he finally lowered the brass instrument and turned to face the tree.

He raised a steady forearm in the air.

At first, Cirrus thought he might be waving or signaling in some way, but then one of the crows swooped down from an upper branch and settled on the man's shoulder, close to his ear, where it proceeded to nibble on the rim of his hat. To Cirrus, looking on aghast, it seemed for all the world as though the bird were telling him a secret.

And then, without glancing round, the man headed back the way he had come—down the long winding path to Black Mary's Hole—while the other birds took to the air and followed silently like a pack of thieves.

⫷ 4 ⫸

The House in Midas Row

Pandora's heart was pounding. No sooner had Madame Orrery drawn attention to her place behind the curtain than Mr. Chalfont had pulled her out of hiding and escorted them into the adjoining study. He rang a little bell to summon a maid and then bent down to check a tag Pandora wore on a chain round her neck.

"Number four thousand and two," he said, walking over to a large wooden cabinet against the wall.

He selected a thick leather ledger from one of the shelves and carried it to a table, where he began thumbing through it, running his fingers up and down the columns of neat handwriting. He came to a stop in mid-May 1771.

"Ah, here we are. Child number four thousand and two," he said. "Female, approximately three days old, in reasonable health." He glanced up from the book and his voice clouded over. "Delivered with a twin brother, later deceased."

Pandora stared at the floor, her ears burning. For a moment she was no longer in the Governor's study, but was standing in a drafty kitchen somewhere in the country. An enormous woman—Mrs. Stockton, the woman employed to be her nurse—lay on the ground in front of her, an empty mug of kill-grief in her hand, while in the corner, still alive, stood a small, sniveling boy, his nostrils caked with snot and his cheeks blotched by fever. . . . Her brother.

The tears came again.

"Good heavens, child. Do not cry!" said Mr. Chalfont, rushing to her side.

She was back in the Governor's study, on a rug before the fire.

He crushed her into his arms, nearly suffocating her, until all she could feel was the edge of his neckcloth biting into her skin. Then he straightened.

"I know. How about some ginger? There is no ill that cannot be cured by ginger!"

He dashed to a slim writing desk by the window and withdrew a small japanned tin from an inside drawer. Pandora could see some of his other possessions, too: a shiny silver locket, a tortoiseshell comb and a peculiar pendant shaped like a globe. A portrait of a woman hung above the desk.

The Governor noticed the direction of her gaze and quickly closed the drawer.

"She was my wife," he said, indicating the oval portrait and holding out the tin in front of Pandora. "She died not long after we were married."

Pandora did not know what to say, but reached into the tin, as instructed, and selected one of the golden nuggets for herself.

"That's right," said Mr. Chalfont. "Now pop it in your mouth."

Pandora cradled the gem of ginger in her hand, treasuring its flame of color, and then placed it experimentally on her tongue. A small fire erupted in the center of her mouth, and her face crimsoned with the unexpected heat.

Mr. Chalfont looked delighted. "There now," he said, dabbing at her cheeks with his handkerchief. "All better?"

Pandora nodded dutifully and turned her attention to Madame Orrery, who was studying a large oil painting above the mantel—a seascape featuring a fully rigged ship surrounded by cliffs of ice.

"*The Voyage of the* Destiny," remarked the woman, reading an inscription on the frame. "An unusual subject for a hospital, is it not?"

"Not at all," said the Governor, helping himself to a large piece of ginger and returning to the table. He pulled a document from a sheaf of papers and started filling in some of the details with a quill. "There was once a time when many of our boys were sent to sea. Several of them even served on the *Destiny*."

"Is that so?"

Madame Orrery turned to watch him closely and then perused the other objects in the room: a spyglass on a nearby table, a nautilus shell on a shelf and a model ship sailing

38

across a desk. Finally, her eyes settled on a row of cabinets against the wall. They were lined with slender drawers, one of which was partially open, revealing a tangled heap of objects inside.

"Tell me, Mr. Chalfont," she said, moving closer. "What do you keep in here?"

Pandora tightened her grip on the scrap of fabric in her pocket, praying the Governor would not discover her theft. She knew exactly what the drawers contained: hundreds of trinkets laid out in trays, each corresponding to a child in the hospital.

"Tokens," answered Mr. Chalfont. "Buttons, rings, bits of folded paper. Anything the poor mothers can find to identify their children when they leave them here at the hospital."

The woman looked up, intrigued. "And is there a token for each child?" she asked.

"But of course. It is a condition of the hospital." Mr. Chalfont set his quill to one side. "Most of the mothers are maids or young women down on their luck when they arrive at the hospital. The tokens they leave are normally objects of personal significance but little value. Something for their children to remember them by, that is all. We record each item here," he said, indicating the ledger on the table in front of him, "on the off chance they might one day be in a position to reclaim them. Their children, I mean, and not their tokens." He pinched the bridge of his nose and gazed into the distance. "Though, I fear, this is seldom the case."

Madame Orrery opened one of the drawers and picked

through its contents. "How . . . tragic," she said at last, dusting her fingers on her dress.

She continued inspecting the drawers while the Governor busied himself with his paperwork.

"And what is it precisely that you do, Madame Orrery?" he enquired after a while, pausing to dip his quill in some ink.

She turned to face him. "I am a mesmerist," she said. "I cure the body and heal the soul. It is a form of animal magnetism."

Mr. Chalfont frowned slightly. "I am afraid I am not familiar with that particular branch of natural philosophy," he said.

Madame Orrery smiled and walked over to the portrait of his dead wife. She stroked the likeness with her fingers. "I relieve the body of its physical suffering and ease the mind of its spiritual complaints," she said. "I wipe the mind clean of its painful memories." She regarded him thoughtfully. "Just one of my sessions, Mr. Chalfont, could alleviate whatever ails you."

Mr. Chalfont stood up and cleared his throat. "That won't be necessary, thank you all the same, Madame Orrery," he said, his cheeks reddening a little. "And now, if you would be so kind." He motioned to the form in front of him. "All we require is your signature and the girl will be yours."

Pandora felt her chest tighten. A hundred words tangled in her throat all at once, all pleading with the Governor not to let her go, but the man merely smiled when he noticed her

40

distress and she looked on helplessly as the woman sat down at the table and wrote her name in a seamless thread of ink.

"Very good," said Mr. Chalfont, clapping his hand on Pandora's shoulder. "Child number four thousand and two, you are hereby apprenticed to Madame Orrery of Midas Row."

A maid arrived with a bundle of clothes, which the Governor pressed into Pandora's hands, and then he escorted her out of the room and down a series of long dismal corridors to the front of the hospital.

"You really must let me see to your gout," said Madame Orrery as he limped beside them.

"That is quite all right, Madame Orrery," he said. "I am content to hobble on as I am. And now, if you will excuse me . . ." He bowed and hurried away.

Pandora watched him go. Apart from a few years in the country, in the custody of Mrs. Stockton, the nurse who had mistreated her, she had spent most of her life within the confines of the hospital—rising early, attending to her chores and caring for the younger girls—but now the doors were opening up and flinging her out. She was leaving the hospital almost exactly as she had entered it: in the company of a woman who did not want her.

She blinked away the light that greeted her eyes and made her way to the gate.

Only once they reached the iron railings separating the Foundling Hospital from the outside world did Madame

Orrery pause to consider her young charge. Her face registered her disapproval.

"What a tiresome girl you are," she said. "Have you no chest? No other belongings?"

Pandora shook her head, her voice taking refuge inside her. What little she owned—apart from the change of clothes Mr. Chalfont had hastily thrown into her arms—she wore on her person. She had not even had time to collect her sole possession from its position beneath her pillow in the girls' dormitory: a prize book Miss Stitchworthy, the instructress, had awarded her for her uncommon ability to read. She glanced at the windows high above her, but there were no friendly faces to see her off.

"Very well, child. Come along."

Two carriages had drawn up to the hospital gate, and Pandora bundled herself inside the one with the silver timepiece enameled on its door. The seats were padded with a thin but luxurious covering of patterned silk, which did little to cushion the hardness of the wood beneath. Madame Orrery squeezed in beside her, her skirts filling most of the space, and the door clapped shut behind them. Immediately the vehicle jolted forward, leaving the hospital in a swirl of dust.

Curled up in her thoughts, Pandora peered through a gap beside the blind at the passing crowds. She had never seen so many people. Everywhere she looked there were ragged figures rushing through the streets: charwomen carrying baskets of coal and tinder, carters transporting barrels, and barefoot children dodging in and out of cart wheels, hitching rides on the backs of carriages. She watched them for a while, envying their freedom, and then raised her eyes to the tops of the tall buildings, hoping for a glimpse of sky, but all she could see were boarded-up windows, cracked tiles and blackened chimney pots spewing smoke.

The city, it seemed, had swallowed them.

Miserably, she groped in her pocket for the piece of fabric she carried with her. Instead, her fingers encountered the sharp stab of metal and she realized with a start that she had failed to return her keys to the Governor. A sudden desire to ask Madame Orrery to stop the carriage and turn round took hold of her. Yet one look at the proud woman sitting next to her convinced her that it was too late. Besides, there was no going back. She was a foundling no more.

With a shiver, she slid even further into the corner of the carriage and picked at the hem of her uniform. Unlike most of the girls at the hospital, she was hopeless at sewing and had twice been confined to the dark room, an airless chamber below the stairs, for cursing whenever needles stung her fingers. What could Madame Orrery possibly want with a girl like her?

Eventually the roar of the streets subsided and the near-constant din of hawkers and ballad singers was replaced by the quieter jingle of the horse's harness and the comforting sound of its hooves clopping against the ground. Madame Orrery finally raised her blind to admit the weak rays of sunlight filtering through the dusty sky.

Pandora's mood brightened. She was greeted by the sight

of creamy-white houses with dark railings and iron lanterns set on slender poles. What the houses lost in height, they gained in girth and grandeur. There was even a private park with stately elm trees in which the residents could wander.

Cheered by this discovery, she dismounted from the carriage as soon as it rolled to a stop and followed Madame Orrery up to a large stone house on the eastern side of the square.

The door was opened almost instantly by a peculiar gentleman in a dove-gray coat. He was no taller than Pandora and dressed in powder-blue breeches, spotless stockings and shoes with prominent heels. Wisps of fine white hair rose like steam from the top of his head. He bowed meekly as they entered and closed the door behind them.

Pandora found herself in a glacial hall with curtained doorways on either side and a floor so bright she could almost see her reflection in its surface. A central staircase curved like a swan's neck up to a small balcony that overlooked the main hall. Two thin doors stood at the top of it, guarding an inner apartment.

Madame Orrery moved beside her.

"The Governor was a buffoon," she declared, her voice booming against the smooth white walls. "Though I do believe he is protecting more than just the boy."

She took two steps up the marble staircase and stopped. A veil of secrecy fell across her face. "One of my private sessions, I think, Mr. Sorrel, will be in order. I must find my way back to the hospital as soon as possible."

The man inclined his head. "As you wish, madam," he said.

"Good. Now show this girl to her room and see that she is put to use."

The man gave Pandora a cursory glance and quickly bowed his head.

"Yes, madam."

Without another word, Madame Orrery walked up the remaining steps and disappeared behind the doors at the top of the stairs. Pandora glimpsed a flash of gold and a streak of mirrors, and then she was gone.

"What is your name?" the man asked her in a high, fluty voice.

"Pandora, Mr. Sorrel," she answered, with a curtsy.

The man's lips twitched in a smile. "Very well, Pandora. Come this way."

Through one of the curtained doorways, she glimpsed a large wooden tub surrounded by a ring of chairs. It was decorated with loose, flowing ribbons and studded with short, elbow-shaped poles.

"What is in there?" she asked, hanging back.

"That," said Mr. Sorrel, sweeping aside the curtain, "is Madame Orrery's Crisis Room. It is where she reveals her healing powers."

Pandora's eyes widened as she took in the fainting couches along the walls. "Is it true?" she asked, remembering what Madame Orrery had told Mr. Chalfont. "Can she really make people's memories go away?"

Mr. Sorrel looked as though she had slapped him across the cheek. "But of course! Madame Orrery is the most celebrated animal magnetist in London. Patients come from far and wide to take advantage of her treatments. It is a most persuasive science. She learned it in Paris from Monsieur Mesmer himself!"

Pandora noticed an odd-looking instrument in the corner. It resembled a small organ, but for the fact that thirty glass bowls, of varying shapes and sizes, had been arranged on top of it.

"Ah, the glass harmonica," said Mr. Sorrel, following her gaze. "It plays the most heavenly music." He flexed his fingers. "That is *my* job: to play soothing melodies while patients recover their wits. And now, if you will come this way . . ."

Carrying her bundle of clothes, Pandora followed him through to the back of the house and up a series of stairs to the attic.

"Your duties will be to clean the Crisis Room each morning before the clients arrive," said Mr. Sorrel, taking short, shuffling steps ahead of her, "and to see to it that the Mesmerism Tub is filled daily with freshly magnetized water." He stopped and eyed her up and down. "I hope you will be strong enough. The bottles are quite heavy and the last girl was not up to the task."

Pandora swallowed the lump of uneasiness in her throat and assured him that she was stronger than she looked.

"Otherwise you are not to disturb Madame Orrery during

her sessions," said Mr. Sorrel. "Her patients are of a highly sensitive disposition and are easily unnerved."

They had arrived at a dingy corridor at the top of the house. Walking to the far end, they entered a shabby room with a sloping ceiling, a tiny grate and a bare bed.

"This is where you are to sleep," said Mr. Sorrel. "There are some bedclothes in the chest, should you require them, and some water in the jug. I shall expect you downstairs presently."

He closed the door behind him.

Pandora stood in the middle of her room, uncertain whether to rejoice at having her own space or to cry at the dreariness of her surroundings. From her window in the girls' dormitory, she'd had an almost unbroken view of fields, but here the only light coming in was from a solitary window, high in the wall, its glass curtained with grime.

She pushed the chest up to the wall and stood on it so that she could see outside. An endless succession of rooftops and chimneys stretched away from her. Almost directly opposite was a small white church tower with the statue of a saint in knight's armor on its ledge. He was piercing the belly of a dragon with a spear. His round shield glinted in the light and reflected what could be seen of the street below. She tried to open the window, but could only raise it an inch.

Dispirited, she got down from the chest and decided to put away the clothes she had deposited on her bed. In addition to an extra pair of stockings, there were two white linen shifts, a handkerchief and a second dress trimmed with red ribbon—the foundling's uniform.

She picked them up and was about to place them in the chest, when something fluttered to the floor.

A scrap of paper.

Her heart lifted. Had Mr. Chalfont written her a letter? Excited, she unfolded the piece of paper, but was disappointed to find the word *Instructions* printed at the top in stern letters.

> YOU ARE PLACED OUT, APPRENTICE, BY THE GOVERNOR OF THIS HOSPITAL. YOU WERE TAKEN INTO IT VERY YOUNG, QUITE HELPLESS, FORSAKEN, POOR AND DESERTED. OUT OF CHARITY YOU HAVE BEEN FED, CLOTHED AND INSTRUCTED . . .

The words started to blur and she skipped a few lines.

> YOU MAY FIND MANY TEMPTATIONS TO DO WICKEDLY, WHEN YOU ARE IN THE WORLD; BUT BY ALL MEANS FLY FROM THEM. . . .

She glanced at the window, feeling like a bird trapped in its cage, and then, unable to contain herself any longer, flung herself on the bed in the corner and buried her face in a pillow that was soon damp from her tears.

❧ 5 ❧

Mr. Leechcraft

"**H**ave you no sense, child? Come here!"

Cirrus, fearing another haircut, dodged to the far side of the table and then ducked as Mrs. Kickshaw lunged toward him. Her hands clapped the air above his head and a shower of flour sieved harmlessly to the ground. Bottle Top nearly fell off his stool; he was beside himself with laughter. High, piggish squeals leaked out of him.

"You can cease your jabbering, you foulmouthed monkey," said Mrs. Kickshaw, who had scrubbed his cheeks so hard they shone. "Do not think I am unaware of your tricks. I can see the devil lurking in your eye!"

She stooped to pick up some buns that had tumbled to the floor and scooped them into the folds of her skirt. As soon as her back was turned, Bottle Top tried to pinch another from a heap that was cooling on the table.

Mrs. Kickshaw was too quick. She planted a vicious smack across his brow.

" 'Tain't for the likes of ye," she said. "They be for good children, who do as they're told. Honestly, you're each as bad as the other. I've never known two such lazy, gadabout boys in my life!"

Despite her outburst, her face plumped into a smile and she turned her attention to the remaining mounds of dough on the table. She began pummeling them with her fists.

"So what did you two boys discover in them fields today?" she said. "Anything of interest?"

"A nest," said Bottle Top. "In the Gallows Tree." He caught Cirrus watching him from under the table and grinned. "There's a bird made of fire in it."

"Is there now?" said Mrs. Kickshaw, only half listening. She flicked away a weevil that was crawling toward the mix.

"And a gentleman, too," said Bottle Top. "Cirrus says he's been watching the hospital."

"What sort of gentleman?"

"A highwayman," said Bottle Top. "He was carrying a pistol!"

Suddenly Mrs. Kickshaw reached down and grabbed Cirrus by the collar. She dragged him, squirming, to his feet. "Is this true?" she asked him, staring fiercely into his face.

Cirrus struggled to free himself, but her grip was too strong. "We didn't get close enough to see," he said, standing on tiptoe and gasping for air. "He was holding something. Could've been a pistol."

Mrs. Kickshaw scowled, then released him. Her skin had been baked as brown as a piecrust from years of working in the kitchen, and her cheeks were burned to a crisp where the pox had scarred her.

"If this be one of your tricks, meant to frighten the young 'uns," she said, "I'll box your backsides to kingdom come!"

"No, mum," said Cirrus quickly. "It's the truth."

He glared at Bottle Top, who was munching on a bun, which he had successfully stolen from the table.

Cirrus hated disappointing Mrs. Kickshaw. She was the closest thing he had to a mother. He had spent all of his early years under her wing and care. He loved the sights and smells of the kitchen: the way bread fattened in the oven, flies quarreled over the milk pails and currants littered the floor like mouse droppings.

Mrs. Kickshaw frowned. "Well, just to be safe, you're not to go larking about in them fields no more. Do ye hear? They're dangerous! Why, only the other day there was a burglary at the Blue Lyon and Molly says that several sheets of linen have gone missing from the laundry."

A bell clattered against the wall and Cirrus looked up, grateful for the diversion. Bells were always ringing at the hospital—summoning them to prayers, calling them to lessons and chasing them off to bed. Bells seldom led to anything pleasant.

Now was no exception.

"That'll be the Governor," said Mrs. Kickshaw. " 'E's been

51

expecting ye. Another master's come to take one of ye boys away."

Bottle Top straightened.

"A new master?" he said, brushing the crumbs from his jacket and running spit-polished hands through his hair. "Why didn't you say?"

"You wasn't here to tell."

Cirrus felt his insides shrink. The last gentleman to visit them at the hospital had taken one look at his unruly hair, tidied especially for the occasion, and dabbed a scented handkerchief to his brow. "Why, sir, a wigmaker must have a graceful and comely appearance," he'd appealed to Mr. Chalfont, who was in charge of the boys' apprenticeship, "of which this boy lacks all but a . . . ah . . . are those devil's horns, perchance, or hair?"

Bottle Top had not fared much better. As soon as he had opened his mouth to speak, the visitor had backed away in disgust. "Whatever do you feed them here, sir?" he said, spying Bottle Top's teeth. "Glass?" Eventually, Aaron had been apprenticed—and only then because his head had been shaved on account of nits.

"Come along, Cirrus!" said Bottle Top, who was at the door, impatient to be off.

But before Cirrus could get away Mrs. Kickshaw had screwed the hem of her apron into his ear and was scrubbing hard.

"There, be off with ye now," she said, dusting the flour from his curls. "Perchance, this time, you'll be lucky."

She guided him to the door and pushed him after Bottle Top, who was already scuttling past the chapel on his way to the gallery, where new masters came to inspect potential charges.

Cirrus took his time, trailing his fingers along the redbrick walls and twirling them round the newel of the giant staircase, which climbed all the way up to the dormitory at the top of the building. At last he came to the Weeping Room, where mothers waited for their babies to be examined for signs of sickness. Jonas had once told him that if you pressed your ear close enough to the door, you could still hear their ghostly wailings on the other side.

"Ah, there you are," said Mr. Chalfont, filling the opposite doorway with his ample frame. "Just the boy I was looking for."

He ushered Cirrus into a room full of oil paintings and curtained windows overlooking the fields at the back of the hospital. Eight boys had been arranged in single file on a rug before the fire, in descending order of height: from Jonas at one end to Bottle Top, wriggling and squirming, at the other. It was like a visit from the Bug Doctor—only, instead of the repellent figure of Mr. Mudgrave, whose blackened fingers inspected the boys each month for lice and nits, there stood a cadaverous gentleman in a purple frock coat with frilly cuffs. He was carrying an amber cane.

Cirrus backed away, instantly taking a dislike to him, but bumped into Mr. Chalfont, who was standing like a father behind him. He clasped Cirrus by the shoulders and positioned him beside Jonas at the head of the line.

"Now then, lads," said the Governor. "Mr. Leechcraft is a gentleman of great learning, a natural philosopher who has traveled to the ends of this earth. He has seen things you can hardly imagine exist. And now he has come to select one of you fine boys as an assistant for his museum in Leicester Fields."

The boys shuffled uneasily and glanced at the impeccably groomed gentleman. Even more startling than his frock coat and frills was the savage necklace that circled his throat: a loop of shells, beads and bits of bone, plus some sharp incisors from an unknown species of animal.

"Sharks' teeth," he said, answering the boys' fascinated looks of horror. His face was long and thin, and crowned by a dark gray wig.

Very slowly, he began to pace up and down the row of boys, swinging his amber cane. "I am looking," he said in a reedy voice, "for a boy to shine like a star in my firmament. To be the attraction in my Hall of Wonders. He must be a child of rare courage, discipline and, above all, Virtue."

Something about the way he said this last word sent a shiver down the young boys' necks.

As if sensing this, he gravitated toward Cirrus and planted his fingers on the boy's head. An odor like the Gallows Tree seemed to hover over him and Cirrus noticed tiny trails of dirt on his skin.

Summoning all of his courage, Cirrus glanced up into the man's face and said, "Begging your pardon, sir. What is a natural philosopher?"

Mr. Leechcraft let out a hiss of irritation and leaned even closer, emitting a blast of bad breath. "A natural philosopher, boy," he said, "seeks to understand how this great Universe of ours works. He studies the forces of nature and apprehends the laws of God." A flash of arrogance lit up his eyes and his voice purred with pride. "It is not for feeble minds to grasp."

He released his grip on the boy's head and continued his inspection of the other foundlings. Then, almost hungrily, he set his sights on Bottle Top, who was staring, transfixed, at the necklace.

"Ah, such a seraphic child. Who could resist such a face?" he said. "This boy, what is his name?"

"Abraham Browne, if it please you, sir," said the Governor, leaping forward. "Though I do believe the other boys call him Bottle Top on account of his teeth."

"And would you say that this child is of high spirits?" asked the gentleman, extending a finger to stroke the boy's cheek, which still shone from Mrs. Kickshaw's aggressive treatment.

"The highest, sir," said Mr. Chalfont. "Why, Bottle Top— Abraham, I mean—is always climbing things. The trees in the garden, the stalls of the chapel. He has even been known to slide down the banister of the great wooden staircase."

Bottle Top's mouth cracked into a grin.

"Though, regrettably for his teeth, he fell off," added Mr. Chalfont, hastily closing the boy's lips.

If anything, Mr. Leechcraft seemed even more pleased by this information. "A brave boy, a daring boy," he said. "Not afraid of a little discomfort." He studied Bottle Top more closely. "His teeth, of course, can be replaced. There is just one thing more I need to consider. His Virtue."

Conjuring a pair of silk gloves from his frock-coat pocket, the man slid them over his hands and began rubbing his cane quite vigorously, until it gleamed in the firelight. Then, with a flourish, he raised it above the boy's head.

The most amazing thing happened. Bottle Top's flyaway blond hair floated straight into the air, as if alive. Thin tendrils curled round the rod and made a faint crackling noise as Mr. Leechcraft brushed it back and forth between the grasping hairs. The other boys watched, astonished.

Mr. Chalfont was not so delighted. "Mr. Leechcraft, I do protest, sir! Whatever are you doing to this poor boy?"

"I am merely determining the quality of his Virtue," said the gentleman. "All of God's creatures are invested with a quantity of Aether, which escapes from their bodies in the form of electrics. Or, as I prefer to call it, Virtue. It is quite painless, I assure you."

Mr. Chalfont's face was a picture of concern. He knelt down and examined the boy minutely. "Abraham, are you hurt? Speak to me, child!"

Bottle Top tried unsuccessfully not to giggle. "It tickles, sir," he said, jogging from one foot to the other. "It feels like there's a spider dancing in my hair."

Mr. Leechcraft's smile widened into a grin. "Splendid!" he said. "This boy will do nicely, Mr. Chalfont. I have made my choice."

56

Cirrus felt a knife twist in his stomach. He had seen many boys come and go during his time at the hospital, but he had never expected Bottle Top to be among them. He had always imagined they would be apprenticed together. What would become of their plans?

He watched helplessly now as Mr. Chalfont beamed into the startled boy's face.

"Well then, Abraham. It appears you have a new calling," said the Governor. "A fresh start in life. You must do everything Mr. Leechcraft asks of you, do you understand? You must serve him well."

Bottle Top glanced uneasily at Cirrus and then nodded his head, too dumbfounded to speak.

"A child who can keep his counsel," said Mr. Leechcraft. "Even better."

He played the puppeteer for a moment longer and then whisked the rod away and tapped it once on the ground to break the spell. Bottle Top's hair fell back into place, though even messier than before.

Mr. Chalfont dismissed the other boys, who gloomily dispersed to their lessons, and then led Mr. Leechcraft, with Bottle Top in tow, to the adjoining study to prepare the necessary paperwork.

Cirrus stumbled to a hard wooden bench outside the Weeping Room and sat down, feeling numb and dizzy. Bottle Top was his only friend, the one always leading him on larks and adventures. How was he going to cope without him?

"Looks like it's just you and me, Flux," said Jonas, strolling past. "The oldest ones left."

Cirrus kept his head down, trying to ignore the sick feeling spreading inside him.

Shortly afterward, Bottle Top rushed up to him. "Mr. Leechcraft says he's going to buy me a brand-new set of teeth," he said, his face shining with excitement. "And some fancier clothes, too!"

Cirrus tried to imitate a smile, but his heart wasn't in it. He wondered how Bottle Top could sound so eager to get away. What would happen to their friendship? He was about to say something when he became aware of the dark-wigged gentleman advancing toward them.

"Come along, you," spat Bottle Top's new master. "We have important work to do. You're going to make my reputation."

He led the boy down the steps to the front of the hospital. Cirrus followed, a safe distance behind, watching as the man's grip on the boy's shoulder grew tighter the nearer they came to the outside world. And then, before Cirrus could say goodbye, he saw his friend disappear into a plain black carriage and drive off toward the city.

Cirrus turned and ran back to the kitchen, alone.

"A quack, if you ask me," said Mrs. Kickshaw once he had told her everything that had happened. "I've heard of his kind before. No better than a charlatan, a rogue! Pshaw!" She spat into the fire. "The Governor ought to know better than apprenticing young boys to scoundrels!"

She caught the worried look crumpling Cirrus's brow and pulled him into an embrace—so tight Cirrus could smell the overpowering stench of her yeasty brown apron. "Now, don't ye worry about Abraham," she said, rocking him back and forth. "He'll find his own way in the world, I promise."

"And what about me?" he asked weakly.

She looked down at him and smiled. "There now," she said, mopping away the tears that had sneaked into his eyes. "Your day will come, too, Cirrus. Your day will come. Someone will come looking for ye, too."

Twelve Years Earlier

THE GUILD OF
EMPIRICAL SCIENCE,
LONDON, 1771

The boat drifts up to the stairs off Strand Lane and two men disembark. One is dressed in a dark blue naval uniform, which fits him snugly round the chest; the other is clad in a heavier fearnought jacket. Above them rises the massive edifice of the Guild of Empirical Science: a crown of architecture on the shore of the Thames, its hundred or more windows lit up against the night by a galaxy of candles.

They each press a coin into the outstretched hand of the ferryman, who stands at the prow, and then hurry up the stone steps, away from the river. They pass through a dim passageway into a cobbled courtyard and from there enter the Guild: an enormous hall lined with columns and marble busts. Blank-eyed visionaries stare down at them from their plinths along the walls.

The two men pay little attention to their grand surroundings, but follow a footman up a wide staircase to the top of the building, where an impressive doorway stands before them. The doors are made of ancient oak, and a godly hand can be seen emerging from a bank of clouds carved into the center of each panel. A Latin motto runs along the top: *Ligatur mundus arcanis nodis*—"The world is bound by secret knots."

The doors swing open and the two men enter a cavernous room filled with blazing light. A long table sits in the middle of the chamber, underneath a glass roof, through which the moon is faintly shining. The table is surrounded by some of the most eminent men in London. There is just one woman.

A man in a red jacket is addressing the table.

"The Breath of God. Think of it, gentlemen," he says in a loud, cannonading voice. "It is the most subtle, elusive force in all existence, the paragon of elements. Many a brave sailor has gone in quest of it. Imagine being able to tap its source, to capture and contain it. Why, we would be like gods! We would have all the power in the world at our disposal!" He bangs his fist upon the table. "We want it, gentlemen, and by thunder we shall have it!"

A gust of wind whips round the side of the building, and the fires that burn in the hearths along the walls roar with their approval.

"But how do you propose to find it?"

It is barely a squeak of skepticism in the large room, but enough to make the man pause, a wineglass half raised to his lips. His eyes search the table until he finds the owner of the small voice: a cartographer in a frock coat with numerous pockets, from which he pulls a collection of tightly scrolled maps.

"The Breath of God is rumored to exist beyond the edge of the world," continues the cartographer, "further than any man has traveled. Venturing upon such an enterprise would be folly, surely?"

The president of the Guild takes a deep breath and returns his glass to the table, spilling a quantity of wine on the tablecloth.

"Folly?" he says. "Then why, sir, are the French, the Spanish and the Portuguese all looking for it? Why do they send their ships to the furthest reaches of the globe? Terra Australis Incognita? Is that what they are searching for? Why, it is but a ruse! They are searching for the Breath of God!"

"But the Southern Hemisphere is ringed by a band of ice and fog," insists the other man. "It is, by all accounts, impassable."

He unrolls one of the maps and spreads it across the table. The paper reveals a filigree of finely drawn lines that dissolve into emptiness the nearer they approach the Antarctic. The bottom part of the map is a gulf of uncertainty.

"Who will guide us to this mysterious Aether?"

The president glances at the door and his lips curve into a smile. "Why, sir, I know the very gentleman," he says. He motions toward the two latecomers. "May I introduce, sirs, Mr. James Flux, First Lieutenant in His Majesty's Navy."

Thirty years old, fresh-faced and clean-shaven, James approaches the table.

Heads turn to greet him.

"Why, sir, he is no more than a boy," says someone on the left, a man with cheeks like marbled cheese. "And certainly no gentleman."

James feels a wave of antagonism surge toward him, but he plows on through the stares of their defiance. His hair is a mass of dark curls, and the buttons on his newly brushed jacket gleam in the firelight.

"Lieutenant Flux, I assure you, is no boy," says the president of the Guild. "Why, in his young career he has already charted an archipelago in the South Pacific and risen swiftly through the ranks of His Majesty's Navy. Indeed, it is said that the wind favors him wherever he sets sail and the sea prostrates itself before him. There is no finer seaman alive."

Someone scoffs, "And who is the oaf in the monkey coat beside him? Surely not some savage he picked up off one of the islands?"

Laughter surrounds the table and James can sense all two hundred pounds of his best friend, Felix, stiffen under his battered fearnought jacket. Together, they have braved the iciest gales and most vicious storms, and he hopes the insults will wash off him now like sea spray.

"Mr. 'Fearnought' Hardy is my second in command," he says, using the name by which his colleague is commonly known at sea, "and a gentleman I would trust with my own life."

One of the merchants dismisses his comments with an idle wave.

"Be that as it may. Kindly tell us, Flux, why we should entrust you with such a mission. You are asking us to invest a personal fortune in your quest for something that may or may not exist. How do you propose to track down this elusive Breath of God?"

"It is quite simple, sir," says James, staring him in the eye. "Because I have seen it."

There is silence around the table—a silence so complete that James can hear the flames sputter on their candlewicks. All eyes are fixed on him, and for the first time he takes in the whole assembly: the proud merchants and tight-lipped bankers to his left, the keen-eyed philosophers to his right, and the heavy-lidded astronomer and clergyman at the far end of the table. Immediately beside James is a silver-haired woman with fine cheekbones and a lofty brow, whose beauty takes his breath away. And to her right sits a shrunken individual, no larger than a child, in an upright chair on wheels.

"I trust you know Madame Orrery and Mr. Sidereal," says the president to him privately.

James inclines his head. "Indeed. I know them both by reputation."

Madame Orrery is esteemed for her investigations into the human mind, which have impressed all of London, and Neville Sidereal, the son of a rich merchant, is reputed to be the cleverest man alive. He has developed an ingenious system of lenses that allows him to see far and wide across the city from a rooftop observatory.

Twiddling a knob attached to the arm of his chair, which

moves a series of cogs and gears beneath, Mr. Sidereal wheels closer. "You have seen it?" he asks.

"Indeed, I have," says James. "The Breath of God appeared above His Majesty's Bark the *Destiny* when I was but a boy and receded into mist the moment I beheld it. Yet I believe I caught sight of its source: a vast continent made of shimmering ice, with the most amazing light behind it."

"What did I tell you?" says the clergyman, leaping to his feet at the far end of the table. "What are the ice caps, sirs, if not the frozen waters of the Flood—that great deluge sent down by God to drown the sinful multitudes? And what of the fog that surrounds them? Why, it can be only one thing—the souls of the departed. Indeed, it is obvious, sirs. The Breath of God resides beyond the edge of the world, at the entrance to the next. Mr. Flux, I do believe you have discovered the very gates of heaven!"

"But have you any proof of this divine Aether?" asks one of the philosophers more scathingly. "Or are we merely to take you upon your word?"

James feels Felix shift beside him.

"I do," he says.

"And would you care to enlighten us?"

"First, I have a condition of my own to make."

One of the merchants, a man with fat ruby rings, snorts. "You have a condition? What, pray, can you demand from us, you upstart whelp?"

James swallows. "A house for my wife and an annual allowance," he says. "She is with child."

For the first time, Madame Orrery displays an interest in the discussion. She leans forward and cups her chin in her hand. "Is that all?" she asks. "You seek nothing else—for yourself?"

Just for a moment, James thinks of his bedridden wife in the tiny room they share in a tumbledown house next to the vile-smelling foundries on the south side of the river. He recalls what she said to him earlier this evening: "Please, James, I wish you would not go. Not for so long, not so far away. Anything could happen. . . . At least wait to see your child."

A blush steals across his cheeks, but he speaks over the doubts and misgivings in his head. "My loyalties are to my wife and child," he says. "I must ensure their well-being, if not my own."

"Very well," says Madame Orrery, her voice hardening somewhat. "I shall see to it personally that your wishes are fulfilled. Now, how do you propose to convince us of this Breath of God?"

"With this," says James.

Taking a deep breath, he loosens the collar of his naval uniform and withdraws a small spherical object from the cord round his neck. It is the terrella he has worn since his first days at sea, the globe engraved with distant countries.

"A terrella?" says the philosopher. "You propose to convince us with a common piece of metal?"

"If you please, sir," says James. "Watch."

He twists the halves of the sphere until they fall into place and the line at the equator cracks open. He glances at

Felix, who, with a slight look of disapproval, signals to the footmen to extinguish the candles. The room plunges into shadow, save for the moonlight drifting overhead.

Very carefully, James removes the northern hemisphere.

The assembled members gasp as a brilliant blue-and-white light escapes from the interior of the sphere and spreads throughout the room, floating in icy waves above them. All at once they rise from their seats and reach toward it.

"It's beautiful," murmurs Madame Orrery, gazing up at the heavenly light. "May I touch it?" She extends a hand toward the sphere itself.

James hesitates, afraid to let go of the sphere, but then slips the terrella into her hand. Immediately, her fingers close round it and snatch the light from the room, sheathing it in a case of skin and bone.

"It's astonishing," she says as a soft sheen takes possession of her face. "I can feel its power working through me. It is like a new lease on life!"

James averts his eyes. He knows its alluring effect too well. He has opened the sphere many times during the intervening years, always surprised to find that the light is still inside, always afraid that the supply will one day run out.

One of the merchants reaches across the table.

"Let me see that!" he exclaims, but Mr. Sidereal is too fast. With astonishing speed he maneuvers his chair closer to Madame Orrery and seizes the terrella from her.

"Such perfect clarity," he says, examining it with a special lens. "Such luminescence. Why, it must be studied!"

"Give that here, you runt," says the ruby-knuckled merchant.

This time, Felix intervenes. Wrestling the terrella away from Mr. Sidereal, he swiftly hands it back to James, who threads the halves together. Gradually, the wonderful light radiating through the room fades and the footmen, until now standing forgotten along the walls, rush forward to relight the candles. Their light seems dull and timorous compared to the brilliance before.

"So," says the president of the Guild, glancing round the table, "what say you, gentlemen? Are we agreed? Do we undertake this mission?"

There is a babble of excited voices, and soon a unanimous decision is reached.

"Good," says the president, smiling smugly. He turns to James. "With our wealth and intelligence behind you, Flux, not to mention the latest instruments to guide your way, our success is assured. Determine the coordinates of the Breath of God—and, if you can, bring back more of this heavenly Aether—and you and your family will be richly rewarded."

Once again, James hears the worried voice of his wife in his ear and glimpses Felix's troubled look beside him, but the temptation to sail is too great. He finds himself accepting the mission instead. "I await your instruction," he says simply.

The president nods. "Kindly see to it that you do not fail. The glory of this nation rests upon your shoulders."

With that, James and Felix leave the room and make their way down the stairs to the front of the Guild. It is even colder now, and very lightly it has begun to snow. Small sleety flakes spiral down from the sky in constellations.

"I do not like this, James," says Felix as they head toward the river. "Did you not see the way they were at each other's throats? It is not safe to give such people power."

"Nonsense," says James. "It will make our reputations."

Felix glances at his friend. "I think ambition is clouding your judgment."

James scowls and listens to the water lapping blackly. "Are you really against me?" he asks, his voice sounding somewhat younger and less assured than before. "Would you honestly prefer to stay behind?"

Felix stares into the distance and for a long time does not answer. Lanterns glimmer on the far side of the river. Finally, he raises the collar of his jacket and stomps his boots against the ground, dislodging the little caps of snow that have formed there.

"You know better than to doubt me," he says, his frown lightening a little. "I shall remain by you to the end. I only wish I knew where that end might be."

Twelve Years Later

LONDON, 1783

❧ 6 ❧

The House of Mesmerism

*P*andora stepped closer to the body on the floor. The woman lay exactly where she had fallen the night before; her mouth was open and a sickly odor emanated from her clothes.

Pandora listened carefully, expecting to hear a breath or a snore, but there was nothing. Not a sound. The woman's lips were parted in a silent roar. And then a fly settled on the woman's cheek and began to crawl across the unblinking surface of her eye, and Pandora suddenly knew the truth: Mrs. Stockton, her nurse, was dead. The gin had finally killed her.

She walked over to the boy who was watching her from a bed of straw in the corner. He was her age exactly, nearly five and a half years old, but so slight and frail he seemed to be fading already into a ghost. His cheeks were swollen and he was whimpering with cold. She took him gently by the hand and guided him toward the door.

Perhaps the woman in the next farmhouse would know what to

do. Perhaps she would take them in and be their mother. Or, if not, perhaps she would take them to that place Mrs. Stockton was always grumbling about, the place they had come from: the "fouling hospital" in London, all those miles away. . . .

Pandora's eyes cracked open. No! She would not think of him again. Little Hopegood, her brother, was dead. She had seen the Governor burying him in an unmarked grave outside the hospital walls. She had failed to save him.

With a shiver, she rose from her bed and stepped across the room to the window. She could still feel the wet suck of mud underfoot as she trudged through the country lanes and the weak, tepid grip of her brother's fingers as they slowly slipped from her own. . . . If only there was something more she could have done.

She climbed onto the chest below the window and looked out, trying to dislodge the memory from her mind. A foul-smelling haze had settled over the city, and the sun was a pale blister, seeping through the cloud.

She got down from the chest, took off her dream-rumpled nightdress and pulled on her coarse brown foundling's uniform. Then, turning away from the window, she left the room.

Mr. Sorrel was in the kitchen when she joined him downstairs.

"How did you sleep?" he asked her as she crossed to the iron cistern against the wall.

"Not well. I dreamt of my brother again." She splashed some cold water onto her face. "I cannot seem to get him out of my mind."

"You ought to let Madame Orrery see to your dreams," said Mr. Sorrel. "One of her treatments would rid you of your obsession with the past."

Pandora glanced at him, curious to know what he meant, but then gave a little shudder. "No, thank you," she said. She was still not certain what went on behind the curtains of Madame Orrery's Crisis Room, but she had heard far too many shrieks and groans during the past few weeks ever to want Madame Orrery to treat her.

Mr. Sorrel said nothing, but spooned some lumpy porridge onto a plate. He sprinkled it with a handful of currants and passed it to Pandora.

Pandora sat down at the table and began to eat, watching as Mr. Sorrel flitted about the room, unable to settle. Even though she had shared with him plenty of details about her past, going so far as to tell him about her twin brother, he had never disclosed anything about himself.

"Tell me about Madame Orrery," she said, trying again to get him to talk. "How did she come to be a Mesmerist in London?"

Mr. Sorrel looked at her for a moment and then sat down. He glanced behind him, as though afraid Madame Orrery might be there to overhear, and then said in a confidential whisper, "Madame Orrery was once the most admired woman in France. She was renowned for her beauty, intelligence and charm. Together with her husband, she attended the most splendid courts and salons."

"Her husband?" asked Pandora, surprised.

"Indeed," said Mr. Sorrel. "Her husband was a renowned clockmaker, the finest in the land."

Pandora remembered the silver timepiece she had seen in Madame Orrery's possession. "Her pocket watch," she murmured.

Mr. Sorrel nodded. "It was a gift from him. A heart-shaped silver timepiece reputed never to need winding, never to lose time. It was meant to be a token of his undying love."

Pandora's heart was pounding. "But I saw her winding it," she said. "A few weeks ago, in the Governor's study. What happened?"

Mr. Sorrel blushed. "Shortly after Madame Orrery received the timepiece," he said, keeping his voice down, "she discovered that her husband had created yet another—but in gold—for a maiden nearly half her age. A woman already fat with his child." He averted his eyes. "It is rumored that the moment she learned of his deception, her blood ran cold and the silver timepiece stopped working—as though, like her heart, it had broken. It never functioned properly again."

Pandora gasped. "What did she do then?"

Mr. Sorrel took a deep breath. "She devoted herself to the mysteries of the body; more specifically, the circulation of the blood and the connection between the heart and the mind. Her investigations led her to the miracles of Mesmerism."

Pandora's head was spinning, struggling to make sense of everything she had heard, but then she noticed Mr. Sorrel looking uncomfortable, as though he regretted divulging so much.

"And you, Mr. Sorrel," she asked more cautiously, "how did you come to be in Madame Orrery's service?"

"That, Pandora," he said very softly, staring at the floor, "I cannot tell you."

His gaze shifted to the heavy bottles of magnetized water that were stored in the adjoining room. Pandora's shoulders sagged. She would get no more from him today.

As if reading her mind, Mr. Sorrel said, "Madame Orrery has a clinic this morning. You are to prepare the Crisis Room, as usual, and then scrub the hall."

"Yes, Mr. Sorrel," she answered, with a curtsy, and moved toward the door.

"And, Pandora," he said, reaching out to hold her back, "under no circumstances are you to mention what we have discussed this morning to Madame Orrery, do I make myself clear? It would not do for her to learn that I have been so . . . indiscreet."

"Yes, Mr. Sorrel."

"Good." The man appeared to relax; his face brightened. "Madame Orrery is having her hair prepared this afternoon for a visit to the Foundling Hospital. Once you have finished your duties, you may take the rest of the day off."

Pandora glanced up. "The hospital?" she said, her mind flashing back to the scene in the Governor's study a few weeks before.

A hesitant smile worked its way onto Mr. Sorrel's lips. "Madame Orrery has convinced the Governor to seek a private treatment," he said. "The strange weather, it appears, is playing havoc with his gout. She is to mesmerize him tonight at the hospital."

Pandora's fingers rushed to the bunch of keys in her pocket, the keys she had failed to return to the Governor, but before she could ask any more questions a bell clattered against the wall. Mr. Sorrel jumped to his feet. He grabbed a tray of sugared dates—Madame Orrery's breakfast—and promptly left the room.

Itching with curiosity, Pandora lugged the heavy bottles of magnetized water to the Crisis Room and slowly got to work. Her mind was buzzing. What was Madame Orrery planning? Only a few weeks before, she had told Mr. Sorrel that she must find her way back to the hospital because the Governor was protecting more than just the boy, Cirrus Flux. She obviously wasn't interested in the Governor's welfare. Was there something else?

The Crisis Room was dark and stuffy, and Pandora opened the shutters to let in more light. Once again her eyes took in the peculiar objects around the room. Her gaze alighted on the glass harmonica in the corner. Only the other day Mr. Sorrel had shown her how it worked. Seating himself on a low wooden stool, he had started tapping a melody on a pedal with his foot, causing the rainbow-colored bowls on top of the instrument to spin. Then, to Pandora's astonishment, he had dipped his fingers in a watery solution and passed them back and forth across the whirling mouths of glass. The most excruciating sound had issued forth, a symphony of wails, like yowling cats. It was the most agonizing thing she had ever heard.

"Ah, the music of the spheres," Mr. Sorrel had said, impervious to the racket he was making. "Some say it induces madness in those who hear it, but I think it transports one to a higher realm."

She had just finished replacing the rancid-smelling water in the tub when the first clients arrived. She quickly closed the shutters, scooped up her things and rushed out of the door. From a distance she watched as Mr. Sorrel escorted a stream of fashionable young ladies across the hall. Their beautifully colored dresses trailed behind them like peacock tails on the floor.

A swish of silk made her spin round.

Madame Orrery had emerged from her private chamber upstairs and was descending the marble steps. Pandora ducked into hiding and watched as the woman swept aside the curtains of the Crisis Room and went in. Then, as if sensing the girl's eyes on her, she turned and gave Pandora a hard, icy stare.

Pandora remembered what Mr. Sorrel had told her: on no account were the patients to be disturbed.

At once Pandora retreated to the kitchen and disposed of the water in the yard. From the hallway beyond came the sounds of Madame Orrery's treatment. A mixture of sobs and sighs, pierced every now and then by a scream. This was followed by a shrill, tortured music. Mr. Sorrel was playing his glass harmonica once again.

Listening now, she was overtaken by a sudden desire to know more. Tiptoeing back to the hall, she crept closer to the curtains and peered in.

She stifled a frightened gasp. The women were sprawled on the floor! They were barely moving, barely breathing, as if dead. Madame Orrery stood above them, her silver timepiece in her hand.

Mr. Sorrel rushed out of the room, nearly knocking her off her feet.

"Pandora!" he cried. "Whatever are you doing here? Quick! Get back to work!"

Pandora took another frightened look at the ladies on the floor. "Are they all right?" she asked, following him back to the kitchen.

"Yes, yes. It is all part of the treatment," he said. Beads of perspiration showed on his brow. "We must induce a fever if we are to purge their minds. Madame Orrery will soon revive them."

He grabbed an earthenware bottle from the larder and brought it to the table. He flicked back the stopper and poured a clear liquid into a number of long fluted glasses, which he set on a tray. The fluid popped and fizzed before her eyes.

"What is that?" she asked.

"Medicated water," said Mr. Sorrel. "It acts as a tonic. Do not fear. The patients will recover—and, once they do, they will remember nothing of what has happened. It will feel as if a great weight has been lifted from their minds. All of their painful thoughts and memories will have been wiped clean."

He heaped some sugared dates onto a plate, set it next to the glasses and then rushed back with the tray to the hall. Pandora was about to follow, but Mr. Sorrel gave her a stern, warning look and she fell back.

She examined the bottle on the table more closely. It looked like water, it smelled like water, but a bubble pricked her nose and she jumped back, startled.

A short while later a chorus of voices filled the hall. The women had recovered their wits and were beginning to take their leave.

Mr. Sorrel reappeared. "You are fortunate Madame Orrery did not catch you," he said. "Mesmerism is a subtle art. It does not do to interfere." His eyes swept the floor. "Now, do as you're told and scrub the hall. Madame Orrery's hairdresser will be here shortly."

"Yes, Mr. Sorrel."

Cheeks flaming, Pandora filled a copper kettle and set it over the fire to boil. As soon as it had heated, she poured the scalding water into a bucket, sprinkled it with herbs and sand, and marched with it to the hall. She knelt down in a pool of steaming water and started to clean the floor.

It was hard, backbreaking work. Her fingers were sore and blistered, and the brush left painful splinters in her hand.

She had almost reached the top of the staircase when a carriage drew up to the house. A bell clattered in the air.

Before she could gather her things, Mr. Sorrel had padded over to the door and admitted a plump, middle-aged gentleman in a powdered wig. A boy entered behind him, carrying a box of brushes and loops of hair.

Pandora kept her head low as the entourage passed by, climbing the steps to Madame Orrery's chamber. The gentleman gave her a wide berth, as though skirting a puddle, but the boy seemed to linger. She risked a glance up and caught him staring at the scarlet trim on her foundling's uniform. There was something in his eyes she recognized—a sad, haunted look.

The twin doors opened and Madame Orrery appeared, dressed as usual in her silver gown. "Ah, Mr. Fopmantle," she said. "How good it is to see you. Horrendous weather, is it not?"

The gentleman stooped to kiss her hand. "Indeed it is, madam, indeed it is. Why, it's as hot as Hades outside and just as smelly, I wager." He paused to sniff a perfumed handkerchief he carried with him and turned to the boy. "Now then, Aaron, don't be shy. Bring my brushes. We must make madam even more ravishing than usual."

A smile lifted the edges of Madame Orrery's lips. "And you have brought your new apprentice again, I see," she said, reaching out to stroke the young boy's cheek. "I did so enjoy his tales of the Foundling Hospital the last time we met. I hope to hear more of them now. Come inside."

Pandora, who had lowered her eyes as soon as Madame Orrery appeared, looked up, surprised by the friendliness in

84

her voice. So the boy was a foundling like herself. But what stories did he have to tell?

She watched as the boy followed his master into the lady's boudoir. The door closed behind them. Mr. Sorrel immediately made his way back down the stairs, urging Pandora not to dally.

As soon as he was gone, she rose to her feet and stretched the stiffness from her limbs. Then, hearing voices on the other side of the door, she moved her bucket closer and began lightly to scrub the floor, hoping to overhear what was said.

Madame Orrery's voice was muffled and low. Pandora could make out only a few words here and there. "I must applaud you," she thought she heard the woman say. "The boy I seek is there."

Pandora's heart skipped into her throat. Was Madame Orrery talking about Cirrus Flux?

Pandora pressed her eye to the keyhole, curious to see what was happening, but could make out little beyond the edges of Madame Orrery's skirts. Then she noticed the boy, Aaron, slouching in a chair. He appeared to be asleep. Madame Orrery moved toward him. Something silver glinted in her hand. "Now tell me, Aaron," the woman said. "Have you ever seen a—"

Suddenly she stopped, turned round and advanced toward the door.

Before Pandora could scramble to her feet, the woman was standing over her.

"That will do," said Madame Orrery icily, as Pandora

moved the brush in frantic circles, pretending to look busy. "You may join Mr. Sorrel downstairs. I have no further use of you today."

"Yes, Madame Orrery," said Pandora with a curtsy. Grabbing her brush and bucket, she hurried down the steps, not daring to look back. She could feel Madame Orrery watching her from the top of the stairs.

Her cheeks were burning and her mind was racing. What was Madame Orrery up to?

She dashed through the kitchen and tossed the water into the yard. She then saw Mr. Sorrel heading toward the mews, where the coachman was preparing the horse and carriage for its journey across the city. She ran after him.

"I need to know," she said, the words leaping out of her mouth. "Why is Madame Orrery going to the Foundling Hospital? Is she after Cirrus Flux?"

Mr. Sorrel refused to meet her eye. "Please, Pandora," he said irritably. "No more questions. There are some things it is better not to know."

She stared at him angrily, but could tell that he wouldn't discuss the matter further.

With a sigh, she glanced at the horse and carriage and noticed the silver timepiece enameled on its door. Immediately she made up her mind. If Mr. Sorrel refused to help her, she would find out for herself. She would follow Madame Orrery back to the Foundling Hospital and discover the truth.

❧ 7 ❧

Black Mary's Hole

Cirrus could stand it no longer. While the other boys lined up for the cold bath, he made a break for the fields.

Ever since Bottle Top's departure a few weeks before, he had tried keeping a close watch on the Gallows Tree from the upper windows of the hospital, but there had been no further sightings of the man from Black Mary's Hole. Worse, none of the other boys believed him when he told them what he and Bottle Top had seen. Even Jonas had started calling him a liar. But Jonas had just been apprenticed to a stationer in the city, who needed a boy with fresh legs and strong lungs to call out news to passers-by, and Cirrus no longer had to endure his taunts and gibes. No matter what anyone else thought, he was convinced that someone had been watching the hospital until recently and was determined to find out who—and why.

As soon as no one was looking, he dashed away from the infirmary and scuttled across the lawn, heading straight for the apple tree he and Bottle Top had climbed before. Unusually for this time of year, the leaves were beginning to turn brown and wither; some had even dropped to the ground. A dry, dusty vapor hung in the air.

Before anyone could notice his absence, he hoisted himself into the branches and worked his way across to the wall. Then, using the rope that still dangled over the other side, he carefully let himself down.

He cut across the field. Here and there large shapes broke through the gloom, but he did not stop until he had reached the Gallows Tree, which stood like a bolt of black lightning by the side of the dirt road.

There was no sign now of the nest he and Bottle Top had investigated before. Instead, a pile of sticks and twigs lay broken and discarded on the ground. He raked through them with his foot, but could find no evidence of the creature that had once dwelled inside. Not a feather, not a shell. Even the pellets he had seen the last time had disappeared. Had he been mistaken? Had all of his suspicions been wrong?

A sound caught his ears.

Tap-tap-tap.

It sounded like someone hammering in a smithy and seemed to be coming from the edge of the neighboring field. Black Mary's Hole.

A cold sensation trickled down his spine and he wished again that Bottle Top was with him, to lend him courage and support. He glanced at the mass of ash-gray buildings to the south and wondered how his friend was coping on his own. Then, girding himself, he moved toward the sound.

A trail snaked through the grass on the opposite side of the road and he followed it, knowing that it led to Black Mary's Hole. For a moment all of Jonas's late-night stories came flooding back and his heart started to tremble in his chest. Even more terrifying than the tales of Billy Shrike was the legend of the witch who had once drowned her baby in the dried-up well—the spring that gave the hamlet its name. The long blades of grass had been flattened underfoot, and it looked as if something large and heavy had been dragged along the ground. Nettles, half hidden in the undergrowth, stung him with their fangs.

He came to a river. It was little more than a trickle here, a narrow brook spanned by a rotting bridge, and the water reeked of decay. Rushes grew in clumps along the bank and clouds of midges swarmed the air.

The sound came again, louder this time, from the other side.

Tap-tap-tap.

He stopped. A row of huts stood on the opposite bank, sprouting like mushrooms from the soil. A cold, scared feeling lodged at the back of his throat and he swallowed it down. Then, taking a deep breath, he slowly advanced across the bridge. The boards rocked and juddered underfoot.

The noise came again, from further up ahead.

A path led past the huts to a small clearing in the

distance. Peering nervously from side to side, he followed it, alert for any movement. The huts had long since been abandoned and their windows were nothing more than gaping holes. A black odor filled the air and he inhaled its tarlike scent.

Just before the clearing was a lone cattle shed, a semicircular stone building with mossy walls and a collapsed roof. The sound of hammering was coming from the other side. He stepped closer and then came to a sudden stop.

The beams of the shed were thronged with crows. Twenty or thirty of them, hunched inside, hooded like executioners. He dared not move, dared not breathe, but stood in one spot, rooted to the ground. He half expected them to rush at him in a volley of wings and noise, but they remained perfectly still, watching him with their baleful eyes. Then, slowly, they turned their heads to look at whatever was hidden from view.

Cirrus willed himself closer, taking tiny, timid steps.

The smell of tar was even stronger now, and he thought he could detect a fiery glimmer in the air. Crouching low, he made his way along the wall until he came to a small window on the western side of the shed. Cautiously, he raised his eyes and peered inside, aware of the birds' awful presence overhead.

The gentleman he had seen on previous occasions was inside, stooped over a large wicker basket. A tall T-shaped metal pole protruded from the interior of the basket, and an enormous net of fabric hung above him from the rafters. A variety of instruments dangled from the joists: pots and pans, a compass and even a small anchor. Elsewhere in the shed lay discarded remnants of cloth—just like the sheets Mrs. Kickshaw said had been stolen from the laundry. They had been cut into sections and dipped in a solution that gave them a fine golden gloss.

A fire flickered just out of sight and threw restless shadows along the walls. Every now and then it erupted into a bigger blaze and the man turned his head toward it.

"Hungry, ain't ye?" he said in a rough, gravelly voice, and scratched his brow.

He had rolled up his shirtsleeves as far as the elbows, exposing thick, muscular forearms that were sun-bronzed and covered with strange inky lines. Tattoos. Cirrus had heard Jonas mention them once in one of his stories. A short brass truncheon dangled from a belt round the man's waist. It wasn't a pistol, as Cirrus and Bottle Top had suspected earlier, but something else entirely.

A spyglass.

Cirrus watched as the man suddenly threw aside his tools and stepped across the floor to a canvas sack that had been slung from a nail near the doorway. He pulled out several long thin shadows, each on a bit of string, and tossed them to the fire.

They were rats! Dead rats!

Immediately, the fire crackled and Cirrus saw what might have been a wing of flame flicker across his vision. A raucous screech filled the air—and Cirrus jumped back in terror, sweat coursing down his spine.

He ducked, just as the man glanced toward the window.

"Soon," he heard the man say from the other side. "Soon, Alerion, I promise. We'll go to the hospital, fetch what we came for and disappear for good. No more of this god-forsaken city for us, eh, girl?"

Cirrus sat bolt upright. Who was he talking to? And what was he planning to take from the hospital? He looked across the fields and considered running back to alert the Governor, but then he heard a soft cascading noise from inside the shed and craned his neck to see what had caused it.

The man was dragging the large net of fabric along the ground toward the clearing. Cirrus scuttled forward, along the outside of the wall, tracking his movements.

A wooden scaffold had been erected over the mouth of the well in the center of the clearing, where people had presumably once drawn their water. The man was now using a rope and pulley to hoist the fabric—like a sail—into the air above it. Once this was done, he returned to the shed for the wicker basket, which he hauled outside and tipped at an angle so that the prominent T-shaped pole was placed directly over the top of the well and beneath the mass of fabric. He then proceeded to attach a series of cords from the base of the sail to the edges of the basket, taking care to knot them tightly. Finally, wiping the sweat from his brow, he turned back to the shed and said, "Are ye coming, then? Or do ye expect me to get this contraption off the ground without ye?"

Cirrus froze, terrified that he had been seen, but then

92

realized that the man was speaking to whoever—or whatever—was still hidden in the shed.

A ball of flame shot out of the building and circled round the clearing before settling on the iron perch above the basket. Cirrus staggered back and sucked in his breath in amazement. It was a bird made of fire! But that was impossible, surely?

He rubbed his eyes and then stared even harder at the fierce, flaming creature. The bird was flickering all over with gold and crimson feathers. It burned so brightly it was painful to look at, but was so dazzling in its beauty it was difficult to look away. Even the crows had gathered overhead, silently watching.

The man had donned a pair of thick leather gloves and was stroking the bird's gleaming breast with his fingers. "Aye, that's my girl," he said. "How about we give them wings of yours a stretch, eh? No one'll notice us in this weather."

The bird screeched in reply—a loud, piercing shriek that made Cirrus want to cover his ears—and then began to fan its wings, sending huge gusts of flame into the air. The crows broke into applause.

To Cirrus's amazement, the fabric above the basket started to bulge and flutter, as though someone were trapped inside it. And then very slowly the basket lifted a few inches off the ground.

Cirrus gripped the wall of the shed, disbelieving his eyes. What sort of magic was this? Could he be dreaming? He pressed his forehead against the stone, trying to control his racing thoughts, but then became aware of an awful silence.

The bird had stopped fanning its wings, and the crows, too, had grown abruptly quiet. The man was staring in his direction.

For a terrible moment their eyes met and then, before Cirrus could get away, the man took several lunging steps toward him.

"It's you!" he shouted. "Come to disturb my bird again, have ye?"

Cirrus stumbled backward and tripped over a bit of rubble behind him.

"No, sir," he said, as the man bore down upon him. "I was only looking, honest."

"Well, I'll teach you to mind your business," said the man, grabbing Cirrus by the collar and lifting him off his feet.

Cirrus could see now that the man's face was covered in yet more inky markings, just like the tattoos on his arms. Cirrus was shaking in terror.

"Poking your nose in where it don't belong!" hollered the man. "I'll show you what—"

Suddenly, he stopped and a different expression came over his face. His brow furrowed and he squinted at the tag that Cirrus wore round his neck. His foundling's medallion, a little brass disk embossed with the image of a lamb. Unlike the other boys in the hospital, however, Cirrus had never been issued a number.

"Well, I'll be . . . ," said the man softly, loosening his hold a little. "You're him, ain't ye?"

Cirrus managed to wriggle free, aware of the eagle-like bird watching him from the clearing and the crows perched ominously overhead.

"I don't know what you mean, sir," he said, glancing behind him at the dry rutted path that led to the bridge. He wondered if he could reach the fields before the birds had a chance to attack him.

The man took a couple more steps toward him. "Now, don't be afraid," he said, moving slowly. "I ain't going to harm ye. All I want is—"

But Cirrus had already spun round and was hurtling down the path as fast as his legs could carry him. He was aware of the man's footsteps thundering behind him, but they soon fell back, and even the crows that had exploded noisily into the air did not pursue him.

Heart pounding, he galloped across the bridge and over the field toward the Gallows Tree, the long grass whipping at his legs and the foul air streaming past his cheeks.

He looked back just once, as he neared the old dirt road, but there was no sign that the man from Black Mary's Hole was following him. Still, he did not let up until he had reached the back of the hospital and scurried up the rope to the top of the wall. Then he quickly dived over the side and joined the other boys, who had finished their cold baths and were heading to the chapel.

8

Across London

Pandora twined her fingers round the bars of the iron railing, waiting. She had fooled Mr. Sorrel by pretending to return to her room earlier that evening, but had quickly doubled back and crept outside. Following the mews round to the front of the house, she had ducked into hiding next to the park in the middle of the square.

Beside her, in the garden, roses exhaled, filling the air with a sweet dusky scent. There was no breeze. Even so, she found herself shivering. After the grueling heat of the day, the night had turned cold and mist hung in veils between the lanterns that shone outside some of the houses.

At last she heard the jingle of a harness and saw the lumbering form of the horse and carriage drawing near. The horse snuffled and snorted, tossing its head from side to side, as though it could sense her hiding nearby, but the coachman took no notice and grabbed a gilded lantern from the front of the carriage as soon as it came to a stop. He advanced toward the door.

Madame Orrery appeared in a patch of golden candlelight and glided down the path. Her hair had been generously powdered and a fur stole draped across her shoulders like a layer of freshly fallen snow.

Pandora watched as the coachman opened the carriage door for the woman and saw her comfortably inside. Then he worked his way to the front of the carriage, replaced his lantern and picked up the reins. He clicked his tongue and the horse quickstepped into motion, slipping on the cobblestones.

Immediately, Pandora propelled herself into action. She rushed out of the shadows and grabbed onto the back of the carriage, just as it threatened to pull away. It was harder than she had imagined. The carriage gave a rough, unexpected jolt that nearly threw her to the ground, but she managed to cling onto a projecting metal rail and carefully brought her feet up off the road. A small platform lay between the wheels and she dug her heels onto it, gradually sinking into a safe, squatting position—exactly as she had seen the street urchins do on her first trip across the city.

The carriage swiftly gathered pace, barreling toward St. Giles's. Several times she almost fell off, grimacing as the wheels thundered over the paving stones, but she gritted her teeth and held on. Unlike the body of the carriage, which was finely sprung, the platform rocked and juddered. Her bones shook, her fingers throbbed and vibrations traveled up and down her arms and legs. Her dress was soon splattered with filth from the refuse that littered the roads.

Deeper and deeper into the city they drove until she began to lose all sense of direction. Small fires glimmered in the lanes between buildings and she could see ragged figures hunched in doorways or else crammed under stalls. Night watchmen prowled the streets, poking their lanterns into shadows, telling troublemakers to move on. She made herself as small as possible, hoping to remain out of sight, and if anyone noticed her they didn't call out.

Finally, the road widened and Pandora found herself on an avenue she knew quite well: the broad thoroughfare leading up to the hospital. She could see the dark buildings huddled behind their protective stone walls and was surprised by the feeling inside her. She had missed the hospital far more than she had realized and longed once more to be within its halls.

She jumped off the carriage as soon as it slowed to a crawl and stole across the street to a smelly yard in which to hide. Large mounds of ash had been piled around the enclosure and clouds of dust swirled before her eyes.

From the safety of her vantage point, she watched as the carriage drew to a halt outside the hospital gates and a white-haired figure, carrying a lantern, appeared. The Governor. She recognized him from the way he limped as he escorted Madame Orrery up the drive.

Pandora tripped over a sudden difficulty. How was she to

get inside? The porter had just taken up a position beside the gates and was chatting amiably with the coachman, who had pulled up the collar of his long brown riding cape, as if to wait out the night. Light drizzled from a lantern in between them.

Pandora clenched the fistful of keys in her pocket, wondering what to do. She was dressed in the foundling's uniform—the perfect disguise—but, unlike Madame Orrery, she could hardly walk up to the porter and demand her way inside. Foundlings were rarely, if ever, allowed outside the hospital gates and she would almost certainly arouse suspicion if she tried.

Desperately, she looked around for an alternative. Then, remembering the two boys she had seen sneaking away from the back of the hospital a few weeks before, she scuttled away from the yard, toward the fields.

A large moon hovered overhead, but it was shrouded in mist and cast an eerie glow. Still, it was enough to see by and she could just make out the trail leading ahead of her. She followed it, her laced boots tripping over the uneven ground. Soft mousy rustlings stirred in the dark and she stopped several times to make sure that no one was around. The fields, however, were deserted.

Then, just as she reached the back of the hospital, where the wall turned away, she heard a harsh animal cry. It was unlike any creature she had heard before: a cross between a screech and a howl.

She ducked against the wall and looked to either side.

There was nothing but the hushed grass all around her. Far to the east a dull reddish glow flickered against the sky.

Uneasily, she carried on. It must have been a fox, she thought, trying to calm down. Or a rabbit, caught by something predatory and wild.

At last she reached the back of the orchard, where the boys had climbed over the wall. She could see the tufts of treetops above it. She reached into her pocket and dug out the small brass tinderbox she had been clever enough to bring with her. She struck a light using the flint and steel, and watched the tiny spark flare in the darkness.

There! A thin trail of rope hung like a vine from a nearby branch and she latched onto it before the light had a chance to fade. As quickly as she could, she tucked the tinderbox into her pocket and lifted herself off the ground.

The rope had been knotted into sections, a foot or more apart, and she used them like rungs to help her climb. The wall grazed her knuckles, but she fought off the stings of pain and soon was lying on the flat stone ledge at the top, looking up at the moon.

Anxiously, she turned her head to scan the grounds.

The hospital was wrapped in shadow, but slats of light shone from the westernmost windows, where Mr. Chalfont would presumably be entertaining his guest. Checking the dense thicket below, she reached out for the nearest branch and carefully let herself down, landing ankle-deep in soil.

Wasting no time, she darted across the orchard to the

edge of the lawn. The clatter and clash of pans soon led her to the kitchen, and from there it was a simple dash to the drive.

The entrance was lit by a lantern, its glass long obscured by grime, and keeping close to the wall, out of sight of the porter who was still at the gate, she crept forward and tried the door.

It was unlocked.

She pushed it open and went in.

A lone candle illuminated the hall and she snatched it, using its meager light to peer round in the gloom. A large wooden staircase climbed into the dark. Treading carefully, she started up the steps. The children, she knew, would already be in bed; the hospital was still and quiet.

She paused on the next landing. Wooden benches lined the corridor to her left and a clock ticked solemnly in the corner. Listening hard, she could just make out the murmur of voices from a doorway further down the hall.

She stepped closer.

The gallery was dark and cold. The fancy canvases along the walls were as black as night and most of the curtains had been drawn; firelight, however, flickered in the adjoining room.

Shielding the light from her candle, she tiptoed toward the connecting door and looked in.

Madame Orrery was seated next to Mr. Chalfont before the fire. She was stroking the air with her fingers and urging him to go "back in time, back in time. . . ." Their chairs were almost touching. On a little table beside them lay the silver timepiece.

Pandora could hear its soft, infectious ticking. There was something about its rhythm that perplexed her, something that niggled at her mind: a skip in the mechanism—a momentary lull—that gave her the impression it was ticking backward . . . or was it slowing down?

Pandora tightened her grip on the candlestick, fighting off a sudden drowsiness that was sweeping over her. Her eyes were growing heavy; her thoughts were confused and dull.

It was too late to warn the Governor. Madame Orrery had already risen from her chair and was inspecting the Governor's face. He did not stir, did not blink. His eyes were open, but he appeared to be asleep. Then, with a cold smile, she put the timepiece away and stepped over to the cabinets against the wall—the same cabinets that had attracted her attention before. She began picking through the children's tokens, one by one.

Pandora watched, mystified. What was Madame Orrery looking for? What was so important that she had to return to the hospital? Judging from the scowl on her face, whatever it was eluded her.

Finally, with a hint of annoyance, Madame Orrery grabbed an oil lamp from a nearby table and turned to survey the room. She seemed to ponder the image of the ship above the mantel and then moved toward the Governor's desk.

Pandora quickly ducked back as Madame Orrery started

opening the drawers. She removed a locket, a comb and the small tin of ginger. It rattled in her hand.

Pandora's brow furrowed. Something was missing, something she had seen before. What was it?

And then she remembered.

"The sphere," said Madame Orrery, seeming to sniff the same suspicion from the air. "Where is it? It must be here!"

She put down the tin of ginger and peered into the Governor's eyes.

"What have you done with it, you sentimental fool? Have you given it to the boy?"

The idea seemed to play in her mind. Her fingers twitched the sides of her dress. Then, spying a loop of keys, she reached over and snatched them. "Shall I go upstairs and find him?"

The Governor blinked and Pandora, unable to contain herself, gave a little squeak of fear. Immediately Madame Orrery spun round—

—but Pandora had already fled from the room. She could think of only one thing to do: find the boy and warn him that Madame Orrery was after his sphere.

In a heartbeat she was on the landing, rushing toward the stairs. The boys' dormitory, like the girls', would be on the top floor; she knew the layout of the hospital well.

Footsteps sounded behind her. Had she been seen? She quickened her pace and dashed up the next flight of stairs. Her candle flame flickered, showing her the door just ahead.

She raced toward it.

103

Desperately, she searched through her keys, eliminating all those she had used before, and finally settled on one that was unfamiliar: a large black key with prominent teeth. She inserted it in the lock, gave a little twist and felt the bolt give way. With a sigh of relief, she opened the door and crept in.

✦ 9 ✦

The Dark Room

Cirrus had just drifted off to sleep when the voice found him.

"Cirrus? Cirrus Flux?"

The words slipped into his ear, sneaking into his slumber, but he went on hugging the safe, fleecy edges of a dream. He was climbing the Gallows Tree with Bottle Top. They were high above the fields.

The voice grew louder, more insistent.

"Cirrus Flux?"

It was a girl's voice.

A girl! What was she doing here? Everyone knew the rules: boys and girls were to be kept in separate parts of the hospital, only ever glimpsing each other at chapel. His eyes opened in alarm and he sat up in bed, his dream collapsing all around him. He craned his neck to check the rest of the ward, but the other boys were fast asleep, their snores rising and falling in waves. A light, however, was moving through the darkness toward him.

He blinked, trying to make it out more clearly. At first he thought it was an angel. All he could see was a tangle of copper-colored hair, illuminated by a candle; but then he noticed the plain brown dress the girl was wearing and the familiar twist of red ribbon woven into the fabric, and he realized that she was another foundling like himself. But how had she found her way inside the boys' dormitory? And what was she doing here?

"Cirrus Flux?" she asked again, a flicker of anxiety in her voice.

This time he grunted and the girl rushed toward him.

"Thank goodness I found you!" she gasped. "We must talk!"

Her voice was like a locket opening, giving him a glimpse of the girl inside. She was barely older than himself, he realized, and scared. The light from the candle she carried guttered and she glanced toward the door.

Suddenly she clasped him by the elbow and dragged him to the floor.

"Shhh!" she said. "She's coming!"

For an instant her eyes burned into his, fierce points of light expressing something he could not comprehend. Like amber, they seemed to trap remnants of her past: hard, hidden tears.

"Who's coming?" he said, but she turned her head to

listen and extinguished all of his questions like the flame, which sent the room gushing into darkness.

Cirrus listened, too. Apart from the relentless thud, thud, thud of blood in his ears, he was aware of the tread of footsteps rising up the stairs. They were too soft to be the Governor's. They crossed the landing and stopped outside the dormitory.

His eyes flitted to the dark wooden door the Governor always took care to lock with his key. A square of light was slowly seeping round its edges, squeezing in through the cracks.

The girl beside him stiffened. "I forgot to lock it," she whispered, as two pegs of shadow grew in the hollow at its base.

The handle began to turn.

Unable to resist, he watched as the door inched open and a woman in a long silver gown looked in. One of the shutters was partially open and moonlight dusted her skin.

Cirrus sucked in his breath; the girl's fear was contagious.

Slowly, carrying an oil lamp, the woman entered the room and moved from cot to cot, occasionally stooping to examine the tags the boys wore round their necks. Instinctively, Cirrus fingered his own metal disk. He was the boy without a number, the boy who did not exist. . . . A few of the other boys mumbled in their sleep, but none of them awoke.

The girl's fingers tightened round Cirrus's wrist. She pulled him even lower to the floor. They were out of range of the woman's light here, hidden behind his bed. Then, as the woman drifted closer, the girl tapped him on the shoulder and started creeping toward the door, round the perimeter of the room.

Cirrus followed, careful not to make a sound, but then looked up as a small figure in one of the beds sat up and wiped the sleep from his eyes.

Cirrus's heart leapt into his throat. It was Tobias!

"Are you a ghost?" said the little boy in a voice that was still half asleep.

The woman stopped and turned toward Tobias, devouring him with her shadow. "No," she said. "I am not a ghost. I am perfectly real."

She placed her oil lamp on the ground and pulled a silver object from her gown. She opened it. The instrument made a soft ticking noise that seemed to fill the air.

"Would you like to see it?" she asked the boy.

Tobias nodded.

The girl tapped Cirrus on the elbow, urging him not to listen. She had cupped her hands over her ears and then continued creeping along the floor. She was heading for the windows, which would give them a clear run at the door.

Cirrus followed, but then, unable to bear the suspense, looked up once more.

Tobias was staring deep into the woman's eyes. His breathing had slowed, his eyelids had sagged and then his head drooped back onto his pillow. The woman gave a little smile and pulled the sheet up over him, then folded it back in a strange maternal gesture. Cirrus shivered.

The girl was urging him to hurry. He started creeping after her once again.

A voice halted him in his tracks.

"I can hear you," it said.

Cirrus froze.

The woman was standing in the middle of the dormitory, surrounded by rows of matching beds.

Instantly, the girl raced back, seized Cirrus by the arm and propelled him toward the doorway. Before the woman could gather up the folds of her gown and give chase, they were hurtling down the staircase.

Cirrus peered madly all around him. Where was the Governor? Why was no one coming to assist them? They were taking the stairs two at a time, nearly tripping in their haste. He clutched the wooden banister to his left, trying to keep from falling down, dimly aware of the light from the woman's oil lamp scratching the walls behind them.

At last they spilled out into the hall and the girl rushed toward the front door. Barely pausing for breath, she flung it open and then, just as quickly, whisked him back.

"What're you doing?" he gasped, as she pulled him into a nook of shadow behind the staircase.

She clamped her hand over his mouth and, moments later, he saw the woman step right past them. She strode out into the darkness. They heard her footsteps peck at the paving stones and then recede into the distance.

Finally, the girl released him and motioned him toward a tiny closet beneath the stairs. Cirrus had never noticed it before. How had she known it was there?

"Quick! Inside!" she said, bundling him into the narrow space.

The closet was cold and dirty, barely large enough for him alone, but she squeezed in beside him and closed the door, sealing them in total darkness. He could feel her breath, hot on his cheek, and the tickle of her hair.

"Stop fidgeting!" she hissed, as something small and spidery crawled across his foot. "Madame Orrery must not find us."

"Madame who?" said Cirrus, not understanding, but the girl simply pressed her hand to his mouth and continued listening to the silence.

And then he felt her give a little shudder. Footsteps were scrunching back toward the hospital. The girl leaned even closer—so close he could smell the tang of sweat on her clothes.

Moments later, a light drifted back into the hall and he heard the woman pacing back and forth, just outside their hidden doorway.

Lamplight sifted through the crack under the door and he stiffened. His heart was battering against his ribs and he wondered if the girl could feel it. Cirrus held his breath and kept very still, afraid that any movement might betray them. Then the floorboard shifted slightly and he was relieved to see the light fading once more to blackness.

A short while later the stairs above them creaked, one at a time, as the woman climbed to the next landing. They waited until the steps had completely withdrawn and then slowly, gradually, relaxed.

Only now did Cirrus allow himself to speak.

"Who are you? What are you doing here?" he gasped, the questions tumbling out of him. He was embarrassed to find that his voice was shaking. "Why is that scary lady after us? And what did she do to Tobias?"

The girl was quiet for a moment, as if collecting her thoughts. Then she said, "My name is Pandora. I used to be a foundling. I've come to warn you."

Cirrus frowned. "Warn me? Of what?"

"Madame Orrery," she said, her voice dying to a whisper. "My employer. I think she's after your token."

"My what?"

"Your token," said the girl. "It's something your mother or father left you when they gave you to the hospital. Your father, I think. I heard Madame Orrery mention him once before."

Cirrus suddenly felt very dizzy. "My father?" he said. Even in the darkness he could sense her eyes burning into his. "I don't know what you're talking about," he said eventually, pushing the thought away. "I haven't got a father. Or a token, either."

"Yes, you have," said Pandora. "I'm sure of it. It must be important, because Madame Orrery wants it. I think it's a sphere. The Governor may have hidden it in his study upstairs."

111

She gave a little gasp. "The Governor," she said. "I forgot about him!"

Before he knew what she was doing, she had pressed something hard and jagged into his hand—a bunch of keys—and started wriggling back through the door to the hall.

"Where are you going?" he said.

"To wake the Governor. I'll be back in a moment."

"Wait! I'll come with you," he said, and made as if to follow, but she pushed him back into the closet.

"No. Stay here," she said. "There's no telling what Madame Orrery might do if she finds you."

She shut the door behind her. Reluctantly, Cirrus did as he was told. He closed his eyes and sank to the floor. His mind was teeming with questions. His father? A token? And now a strange woman was looking for him, too—and possibly the man from Black Mary's Hole. . . .

He sat back, hunched in thought, waiting for the girl to return.

Only, she didn't.

⊰ 10 ⊱

The Silver Timepiece

Gripping the banister, Pandora started up the staircase, guided only by the slivers of moonlight shining through the windows. Everything was black or tinged with silver. She could barely see without a candle.

She listened carefully. The clock on the landing was ticking above her. But where was Madame Orrery? Was she still hunting for them? Or had she returned to the Governor?

The stairs suddenly gave way to smooth ground and she stumbled across the landing. Finally, after what seemed like ages, she found the door to the gallery and sneaked inside. Light flickered from the adjoining study and she tiptoed toward it. Cautiously, she tilted her head and peered in.

The Governor was seated just as before, in an armchair before the fire. He had not moved. His hands were neatly folded in his lap and his short legs barely touched the floor. There was no sign of Madame Orrery.

Pandora rushed over to him and waved her hands in front of his eyes. "Mr. Chalfont! Wake up," she said, as loudly as she dared. "I need to speak to you. It's important."

His eyes were open, but if he saw her he gave no indication.

She shook him by the arm.

"Mr. Chalfont, please," she said again. "It's Madame Orrery. She's after a token. I think you know where it is."

Still, he did not respond. His breathing was slow and quiet; in fact, he hardly seemed to be breathing at all.

"Can you hear me?" she cried, in despair.

This time, he blinked.

Her heart gave a little leap of joy.

But instead of looking at her directly, Mr. Chalfont seemed to focus on something just above her head. She spun round and saw the portrait of his wife hanging on the wall.

"Elizabeth?" he said in a distant voice. "Is that you?" Like a blind man, he reached out to touch her face.

She jumped backward. "No, Mr. Chalfont. It's Pandora," she said. "Child number four thousand and two."

He showed no sign of comprehension.

"Elizabeth?" he said again, his voice rising now like a frightened child's. "Are you there? Oh, Elizabeth, how I've missed you!"

Pandora glanced around her, afraid the sound would attract attention.

114

"Mr. Chalfont, please," she said, fighting to control her voice. "Madame Orrery is looking for a token. I think it belongs to Cirrus Flux. I need you to help me find it."

But Mr. Chalfont seemed to sink into desolation. "Gone," he said sadly. "Gone, my Elizabeth, gone."

Pandora groaned. And then suddenly a thought occurred to her. What did Mr. Sorrel use to revive Madame Orrery's patients?

She looked round the room for a glass of water and her eyes alighted on the tin of ginger. "There is no ill that cannot be cured by ginger," she remembered the Governor saying. She leapt to the desk and was just about to open the tin when she became aware of another presence in the room.

A sigh of silk behind her.

Slowly, fearfully, Pandora turned round and saw Madame Orrery watching her from the doorway. The silver timepiece glinted in her hand.

Pandora almost collapsed; her legs buckled under her. There was no escape this time. She was well and truly trapped.

"Ah, there you are," said Madame Orrery. "I was wondering where you had got to. What, I wonder, have you done with the boy?" Her eyes searched the room. "I saw you with him earlier. Is he near?"

Pandora shook her head, trying to think of something to say, something that might deter her. "I told him to run away," she said quickly. "He jumped over the wall and escaped."

Madame Orrery studied her closely, her brow wrinkled with suspicion. Pandora realized to her horror that the woman's fingers were reaching for her silver timepiece.

Just then Mr. Chalfont started to stir. He was making a soft moaning noise like some of the patients in the Crisis Room. Was he waking up?

"What's wrong with him?" asked Pandora, hoping to distract the woman.

Madame Orrery's eyes flitted to the Governor.

"He will wake," she said, apparently unconcerned. "In time. But he will not remember any of what you have told him. He will only marvel that his gout is better."

"And me?" said Pandora nervously. "What will you do with me?"

Madame Orrery returned her gaze to the girl's frightened face and her expression hardened. "That depends," said Madame Orrery, "on whether you help me now. Where is the boy?"

Pandora put down the tin of ginger.

"I told you," she said, taking a step backward. "He—"

Suddenly, she stopped. For the first time she noticed how cold the woman's eyes were: a cruel, malicious blue. Like ice, they seemed to trap her in their stare. Madame Orrery was waving a finger in the air. Pandora could not break its spell. Fear flickered in her chest.

The silver timepiece had started ticking and Pandora could hear its slow, suggestive rhythm.

"Where is the boy?" asked Madame Orrery again.

The voice seemed to come from far away. Pandora was having difficulty concentrating. Her thoughts were muddled and confused. A numbing whiteness was seeping into her mind like mist, making her feel sleepy and light-headed. And still the silver timepiece went on ticking. . . .

"Where is the boy?"

The image of Cirrus Flux, hidden beneath the stairs, flashed into her mind and she was about to respond, but then she saw a different face, a younger boy. Her dead twin brother. She saw him with such startling clarity, it took her breath away.

"What boy?" she muttered feebly.

"The one you are protecting."

A tear rolled down her cheek.

"Where is he?"

The memory came flooding back. Hopegood following her through the country lanes. Only, she was lost and it was dark and she could not find her way to the next farmhouse. The boy would not stop whimpering; he was shivering with cold. Finally, she had to leave him against a drystone wall while she went to look for help, trudging up and down the muddy lanes.

Pandora wanted to run back and rescue him, to tell him that she had not forgotten, but she felt so tired and her legs would not move.

"He's gone," she said faintly.

"And does he have the sphere?"

All Pandora wanted was to sleep. The mist was spreading all around her, sapping her of energy. Her eyelids were closing, her head was drooping.

Before she could answer, it had rolled forward in a nod.

Twelve Years Earlier

LONDON, 1771

The figure staggers down the twilit street, barely conscious of where he is going. Coaches and carriages rumble past, kicking up a filthy spray, but he carries on through the driving rain, willing himself away from the scene he has just witnessed.

"Is 'e ill, d'you reckon?" says a woman from the doorway of a nearby shop.

"Nah. Drunk, more like," says her companion, a red-haired woman in tattered lace. "Either way, 'e don't look long for this world, now do 'e? Pity, seein' as 'e's so young and 'andsome and all."

The two women turn their attention to the other figures passing up and down the crowded street. The man could be fatally wounded for all they know, but neither can guess at the extent of his injury. There is a scared, haunted look in his eyes, as if Death is just around the corner.

A few minutes later, a boy detaches himself from the shelter of a ledge, under which he has been keeping dry, and falls into step beside him.

"Need a light, sir?" he says, blowing on a torch to keep it aflame. The light gleams on his hopeful face, washed clean in places by the rain.

The man shakes his head and moves on.

"You all right, sir?" says the boy. "I can guide you anywhere you need to go. From Holborn to Shoreditch, Marylebone to Chelsea . . ."

"No," says the man. "Leave me be."

"Honest, sir—"

"I told you. Leave me be!"

The boy stops. His torch sinks slowly to his side.

Relenting a little, the man glances back, digs out a coin and tosses it to the child. The boy palms it hungrily and speeds off down a neighboring alley.

The streets are slick with mud and the man slips on the paving stones, nearly falling, but he manages to right himself and keeps going, stumbling toward the outskirts of the city.

Finally, he rounds the corner of Red Lyon Street, the dimly lit thoroughfare leading up to the gates of the Foundling Hospital. He can see it in the distance, a boundary against the fields. Two brick buildings stand inside the gates, edged by covered walkways. He scans the row of windows, searching for the room in which he used to sleep, but his mind is a blur of memory and he cannot find it.

An iron railing runs across the front of the hospital, lit by a solitary lantern. The flame is barely bright enough to illumine the crest beneath: a woolly lamb standing on top of a shield in which a naked child reaches out for help. A bell hangs nearby and the man grabs it, clanging it more forcefully than intended. The noise rends the silence and a dog barks somewhere in the distance, chasing echoes through the night.

A wedge of light appears from the doorway of a lodge inside. A man with stippled gray hair appears. He is dressed in a wrinkled nightshirt. He shuffles across the rain-soaked drive, looking like a grumpy hedgehog.

"Will ye be quiet, for heaven's sake?" he hisses, as the man continues to ring the bell. "Ye'll wake the children if ye're not careful."

The porter holds up his lantern and inspects the young man on the other side. He is a naval officer, by the looks of it, in a sodden blue uniform. Abundant curls are plastered to his brow.

"Sorry, sir, but there ain't no room," he says finally, motioning toward the little bundle the man cradles under his coat, the precious cargo he has been carrying across the city. "We've too many mouths to feed as it is."

"Please," says the officer. "You must help me. My wife. She's—she's—" He cannot bring himself to say the word.

"Ye'd best come back when we've got a place," says the porter sadly. "We'll post a sign as soon as we are able."

The officer's heart sinks. He knows all too well about the hospital's system of admissions. It is a lottery. He has seen mothers lining up to pull colored balls from a sack, each deciding the fate of a newborn child. A white ball means the child can be admitted, subject to a medical examination; a red ball means the child is put on a waiting list; a black ball, and the child is turned away. There are far more babies than places available.

"Please," he says, reaching through the bars of the iron gate and clinging to the other man like a prisoner. "It is a matter of life and death."

"It always is, sir. It always is."

"But I cannot wait," says the officer. "My ship sets sail tomorrow. Summon Mr. Chalfont. Tell him—"

"Mr. Chalfont?" says a lady, who has emerged from the lodge behind them. She stops when she sees the dark-haired officer.

"James?" she says, rushing forward to take a closer look. "James Flux? Is that you?"

A bashful smile creeps over the young man's face and he shifts from one foot to the other. Years have passed, but there is no mistaking the woman who once cared for him as a child. She was just a slip of a maid back then, but now her bosom has filled out and her waist expanded. Still, her face is the same, kind and considerate, marred only by the pockmarks on her skin.

"Come, come, man," she says, clobbering the porter with her fist and nearly grabbing the ring of keys from his hand. "Let him in, Mr. Kickshaw, and be quick!"

Unconsciously, she tucks a lock of fading brown hair

beneath her muslin cap. "Well, I'll be. James Flux," she says. "I'd recognize those devil's curls anywhere! Sweet Jesus, how ye've grown!"

She pulls James into an embrace, but then, just as quickly, holds him back. "Lord Almighty," she says, her eyes coming to rest on the bundle under his coat. "What've ye gone and done?"

"Please," says James, his voice cracking. "I must speak to Mr. Chalfont. It's Arabella. She's—"

Once again, he cannot bring himself to say the word. The crestfallen look on Mrs. Kickshaw's face, however, tells him that she has guessed it.

"Follow me," she says, grabbing the lantern from her husband's hand and steering James toward the entrance.

The porter shuts the gates behind them.

"Poor Arabella," says Mrs. Kickshaw as they pass down one of the covered walkways. "She was such a good-natured child. Did she live to see the baby?"

Miserably, James shakes his head.

"Poor Arabella," says Mrs. Kickshaw again, this time making the sign of the cross.

She opens a door and they enter a dark hall. The quiet is broken only by the ticking of a clock above them. All of a sudden memories crowd round him: Felix, fat and heavy, sliding down the banister of the staircase; children marching off in pairs to hear Mr. Handel's latest composition in the chapel; the sound of sobbing issuing from the Weeping Room upstairs. His mind travels back to the cramped closet under the stairs where he and Arabella once hid after stealing strawberries from the garden. He remembers the thud of their heartbeats in the confined space, the sweet smell of her breath, the taste of strawberry on her lips. . . .

"Wait here," says Mrs. Kickshaw, leaving him alone in the darkness.

She climbs the stairs, taking the lantern with her.

Something stirs against his chest. The little weight he has been carrying for miles has started to wriggle, kicking the sleep from its limbs. Carefully, he reaches inside his jacket and brings out the ugly, wrinkled face—a stranger to him still.

"Ah, would ye look at the wee thing," says Mrs. Kickshaw, returning. With practiced hands, she scoops the infant into her arms and cradles it against her chest. "God bless his soul. He's the image of his father."

She places a work-toughened hand on the baby's head and straightens the curl of hair that has swept across its brow. James feels a sickening stab of loss. Just for a moment he thinks of Arabella, wrapped in crimson sheets, and goes numb.

The baby watches him with unfocused eyes and then reaches out to catch the words gushing from the woman's lips: a lullaby Mrs. Kickshaw has sung to many a new foundling. The child snatches the woman's finger in its fist and begins to suck on it, making nuzzling noises in the dark.

"Ah, ye're hungry, ain't ye, poppet?" says Mrs. Kickshaw, cooing over the infant.

"James?" A voice startles James out of his reverie and he

looks up. Mr. Chalfont is peering down at him from an up-stairs landing. "Come on up, boy, come on up. Eliza'll see to the child."

James finds himself following the familiar figure up the stairs and across the landing to his study, while Mrs. Kick-shaw takes the baby to the nursery. The spry little man he once knew has rounded into a podgy figure with fluffy white hair, and James cannot help thinking of the day Mr. Chalfont arrived at the hospital, fresh from the Navy, inspiring the boys with his tales of adventure.

Before long, James is standing before a fire in the Gover-nor's study, surrounded by objects from the gentleman's past. He picks up a shell from a nearby shelf and listens to it, hear-ing a distant echo in his ear. Then he notices the painting of Mrs. Chalfont above the desk and goes over to examine it.

"Tell me, James," says Mr. Chalfont, sinking into the chair before the fire and elevating his gouty leg on a footstool. "Exactly what has happened?"

James feels his throat constrict. His cheeks grow hot. Once again he can see the midwife running back and forth, ridding bowls of blood in the yard and calling for more hot water. Then he remembers his wife's agonizing scream, fol-lowed moments later by the tremulous cry of a newborn in-fant.

And then the silence. More than anything, the terrifying silence.

Tears are flowing freely down his cheeks.

Mr. Chalfont listens patiently while he describes the

scene and neither man notices Mrs. Kickshaw, who has returned with the infant.

"I wish we had room," says Mr. Chalfont finally, "but you know how it is."

"Please," says James. "I do not know what else to do. I have nowhere to go. The hospital is my only home." He is aware of the panic rising in his voice and fights to keep it back.

"I am sorry," says Mr. Chalfont, "but you must try to understand. We have limited resources. There is nothing we can do."

He holds out his hands as if to prove the point, but James cannot accept his answer.

"I can pay," he says suddenly, reaching into his pocket for all the money he has with him. "The Guild has promised me much, much more on my return. This must be enough, at least for now, to pay for his maintenance."

Mr. Chalfont looks affronted. "James!" he says. "You, more than any, ought to know that your responsibility lies with your child and not the Guild. What the boy needs—and deserves—is love. Be a father to him, James. Do not leave him."

James shakes his head. "You do not understand," he says. "The ship is docked at Deptford Yard. I am due to sail tomorrow. . . ."

He thinks of all the preparations the Guild has made, loading the ship with the finest cargo and equipment. He feels the weight of responsibility round his neck and touches his terrella, recalling the celestial light that once hovered above the *Destiny*.

A thought suddenly occurs to him. "I can get her back," he mutters faintly.

"James?" says Mr. Chalfont. "I do not understand. What are you suggesting?"

"I can get her back," he says, with greater certainty. He remembers the icy continent he saw. The very gates of heaven, the clergyman called it. "I can sail to the edge of the world and find her!"

Mr. Chalfont shakes his head. "James, be reasonable, man! You are not talking sense." He turns to the picture of his wife on the wall. "Do you not think that I miss my Elizabeth? I know how it is to lose someone so loved, so cherished. But such is the will of God. There is nothing I—or anyone else— can do to change it. We must accept these things."

But all James can see right now is the glimmer of other-worldly light beyond the horizon. "I must try!" he cries. "At least let me try!"

"But James, think of your son," says Mr. Chalfont one last time, trying to dissuade him. But he can see that James's mind is already made up; there is a faraway look in his eyes.

With a sigh, Mr. Chalfont turns to the child. "At least a token, then, for your son, James," he says. "So that you can return and reclaim him."

James stares at the infant in Mrs. Kickshaw's arms and

chokes back a sudden sob, struck by the enormity of his decision. The child is looking at the silver sphere round his neck and reaching out with shell-pink fingers.

"Give him this," James says, removing the terrella and handing it quickly to the Governor, along with all his money. "It is everything I have. Take them! Before I change my mind."

Mr. Chalfont's eyes are glistening, but reluctantly he accepts the silver sphere and places it on the desk, underneath the image of his wife.

And then, before Mr. Chalfont can prevent him, James flees from the room, rushing past the Weeping Room and tripping down the stairs, not daring to look back, afraid that if he stays even a moment longer he will not be able to leave his son behind.

Above him, the infant starts to scream.

Twelve Years Later

LONDON, 1783

❦ 11 ❧

The Boy Who Did Not Exist

Cirrus woke. He was lying on a hard wooden floor, in a narrow room, his right leg twisted under him. A shaft of light hovered in the air in front of him, threading across the interior like the strand of a broken spider's web.

Tenderly, he rubbed the nape of his neck and sat up, trying to make himself more comfortable in the small, confined space. What was he doing here? Why was he not safely tucked up in bed?

And then he remembered. He was hiding from someone.

The sound of footsteps startled him and he pressed his eye to a gap in the boards—a keyhole—giving him a partial view of the hall outside. Daylight was streaming in through the open windows and he could see Mr. Chalfont pacing back and forth. His wig was askew and his frock coat and breeches looked crumpled and creased, as though he had slept in them overnight.

"Any sign of him?" asked the Governor, as Mrs. Kickshaw joined him.

Mrs. Kickshaw shook her head and wiped her brow. "He ain't nowhere to be found," she said. "I've checked the chapel, the lodge and the infirmary. You don't suppose he's wandered into them fields again?"

Mr. Chalfont wrung his hands and then hung them uselessly by his side. "I honestly do not know," he said. "I locked the dormitory last night, as I always do, but this morning it was open and his bed was empty. How he could have got out, I have no idea."

"The little devil!" said Mrs. Kickshaw. "Wait till I get my hands on him! I've warned him many a time to stay away from them fields! They ain't safe for no one, especially the likes of a child!"

Only slowly did it dawn on Cirrus that he was the boy they were looking for. He was tempted to rush out and surprise them, but the risk of their displeasure kept him back. He remained very still and quiet in his hiding place.

"What should we do now?" asked Mrs. Kickshaw, turning anxiously to the Governor.

"I suggest we keep looking," said Mr. Chalfont. "I have locked the boys in the dormitory and asked the maids to check on the girls, just in case he's up to his father's tricks. You search the grounds, and I'll . . . I'll . . ." His voice trailed off and he peered up the stairs, his face clouded with worry.

"Yes, Mr. Chalfont," said Mrs. Kickshaw, with a curtsy. "I'll ring the bell should I find him."

She gathered up her skirts and bustled out into the yard, while Mr. Chalfont turned and clambered up the staircase, his footsteps passing over the spot under which Cirrus crouched, concealed.

Cirrus relaxed his hold on the closet door and sat back, deep in thought. From the edge of his mind came the fleeting image of a woman prowling round the dormitory, looking for him. She had held a silver instrument, which she had used to bewitch Tobias. And then he remembered the fiery-headed girl. His fingers closed round the loop of keys she had left for him and which had slipped to the floor. Where was she? Why had she not returned?

Heart pounding, he wriggled out of his hiding place and emerged, dusty and disheveled, in the front hall. Luckily, there was no one around to see; he was dressed still in his nightshirt.

He crept to the base of the stairs and listened carefully.

From up above he could hear the Governor's footsteps roaming from floor to floor, searching for him. He waited until the sounds had withdrawn into the furthest corner of the hospital and then, as softly as he could, padded up the wide wooden staircase, keeping close to the wall, where the boards were quietest.

What had the girl said? Something about the Governor's study and a token shaped like a sphere . . .

He made his way across the landing, clutching the keys in his hand, wondering which one to use, but there was no need. The door to the gallery was open and he slipped soundlessly inside.

The curtains had been drawn and the air had a musty smell of tobacco. The fire in the hearth had burned down to a sullen glow and the portraits on the walls were barely visible. There was no sign of the girl from the night before.

He opened one of the curtains to let in more light. If anything, the haze above the fields was even thicker than the day before, and he could already feel the heat behind it, pressing against the glass. Below, in the garden, Mrs. Kickshaw was talking to the maids, who were taking baskets full of washing to the laundry.

The clock on the landing started to chime. He hurried away from the window.

It had been a long time since he had stepped foot inside the Governor's study and he was surprised by the memories stirring within him. There, on a little table by the window, was the spyglass Mr. Chalfont had once jokingly told him showed you the other side of the world when you held it to your eye. And next to it lay a spiky seashell, which sounded like a sleeper breathing in your ear. . . . All of a sudden he remembered the Governor bouncing him up and down on his knee and couldn't resist a smile.

The floor above him creaked and he turned his thoughts back to the present. He wasn't sure what he was looking for, but he started with the cabinets against the wall. They seemed promising.

Each cabinet was lined with slender drawers and, when he opened them, he found all manner of trinkets heaped inside. Buttons, brooches, coins that had been sawn in half and even scraps of paper containing handwritten notes and prayers:

Sirs, have mercy on this child, for I have no means of caring for her. I am not without sin, but she is innocent. . . .

Gentlemen, I have been seduced and reduced by the most treacherous of men. Please, I implore you, accept this child. . . .

His heart started beating faster. Were these the tokens the girl had spoken of? If so, was there one for him?

He rummaged through the drawers, wondering what secrets he might find. Each object was attached to a loop of red string and identified by a number—corresponding, he supposed, to the medallions the children wore around their necks. A sudden doubt pierced him. He was the boy without a number, the boy who did not exist. . . . What if the girl was mistaken? What if there was no token for him?

He continued sifting through the keepsakes, his mind full of troubled thoughts. But each item was already accounted for, labeled with the number of another child, a different child who had been loved, longed for and missed.

Not him.

At last, in despair, he turned to survey the entire room. There were no more cabinets to look through, no more tokens in the drawers. And then he spotted a ledger lying on a nearby table and went over to it, curious to know what it contained.

The pages, each divided into rows and columns, recorded the names and numbers of all the children who had been abandoned at the hospital since its inception many years before. A large proportion of the entries held the words "dead" or "deceased" next to them in faded ink.

He fanned through the pages until he came to an entry he recognized.

CHILD NO. 4,018. MALE. ADMITTED 6 JULY 1771. ABRAHAM BROWNE.

His friend, Bottle Top!

Cirrus took a deep breath and checked the preceding page. Halfway down was a gap—a missing entry—where, he supposed, another child ought to have been. A ghost.

A chill crept over him. There was writing near the margin, but it was faint and hard to read. He carried the ledger over to the window to study the words more carefully. Under the column labeled *Remarks* was a statement: *Father paid £100 for the boy's maintenance. Child to be known as C— F—.*

Cirrus felt a tide of grief and shame wash over him, as though he had been abandoned at the hospital all over again. His heart was pounding painfully and he could barely breathe.

The girl was right: he *did* have a father. But his father hadn't wanted him. His father had paid to get rid of him. He had been given away for a sum of money.

The room dissolved in a mist of tears and he turned away from the window, not sure what to do or think. His legs wobbled under him and he sank into a chair beside the Governor's desk.

A young woman was smiling at him from an oval picture on the wall. She had a kind, compassionate face, with bright green eyes and a hint of auburn hair. He laid the ledger down and stared up at the portrait, longing suddenly for a mother's touch. Underneath the picture was a caption: *Elizabeth Chalfont, 1723–48*.

He glanced at the Governor's desk. It had never occurred to him before that the Governor might have a past of his own—that he might have been married, even. But now that he looked more closely, he could see that the desk was not just a clutter of quills and paper, but a memorial to his wife.

He found a locket in the topmost drawer, with a curl of hair inside, and a tortoiseshell comb. Delicately, he stroked each item, and then he noticed the tin. He suddenly remembered the playful taste of ginger in his mouth and opened it. Inside was a loop of string. Curious, he fished it out and withdrew a small metal sphere.

His heart skipped a beat and a strange tingling sensation passed through him. The sphere was attached to a tag with no number!

He replaced the tin at the back of the desk and rolled the sphere around in his fingers. The surface was encrusted with sticky brown sugar and he wiped it clean on his nightshirt. The sphere was inscribed with the outlines of distant countries. Two words were engraved near its base: *James Flux*.

This was his inheritance, his token of remembrance! He was sure of it. It was just as the girl had said. But why was Madame Orrery after it? And why had it been hidden?

Voices wandered into the adjoining room and he squeezed into the gap between the wall and the door, gripping the sphere tightly, unwilling to let it go. Two figures had entered the gallery and were standing, like duelists, on the rug. Cirrus recognized the Governor immediately.

"It is not my fault," said the little man, his hair sticking up in tufts. "He is just a boy. What else ought we to have done?"

The other man's voice was gruff and low; his back was turned to the door. "You ought to have guarded him more closely. Never let him out of your sight."

A shiver ran down Cirrus's spine. There was no mistaking the owner of the other voice. It was the man from Black Mary's Hole! Peering stealthily round the door, Cirrus could just make out his dark blue coat and the three-cornered hat clenched in his hand.

"Come now," said the Governor. "You were just like him once. A happy, carefree child. What has changed you so?"

140

"I have seen the ways of the world," said the stranger, "and grown up."

Cirrus felt the blood drain from his cheeks. He wanted to flee from the room immediately, but his path across the gallery was blocked. He would have to remain where he was. He hugged the wall and listened carefully.

"The woman," said the man from Black Mary's Hole. "She was here last night. I saw her."

"Madame Orrery?" said the Governor, his voice quavering a little. "No, no, it is not what you think. She was helping me with a private matter; that is all. She is a mesmerist. She was relieving me of my gout."

"She is a damnable woman and not to be trusted," said the stranger. "She has seen the sphere before and will not rest until she finds it."

Cirrus rolled the sphere once more in his fingers, wondering what it was for. It didn't look all that special. Perhaps the metal was valuable? Or perhaps it led to treasure?

"Have you still got it?" asked the man suddenly. "Is it here?"

The Governor glanced at the study door. "But of course," he said. "The sphere is well hidden, I assure you."

"Get it for me now," said the man. "I shall take it with me and be off. It is something I should have done long ago."

"But it is the boy's token of remembrance," said Mr. Chalfont feebly. Nevertheless, he did as he was told and marched the short distance to the desk.

Cirrus stiffened behind the door. The Governor was so

141

close that Cirrus could almost reach out and touch his crimson jacket. But Mr. Chalfont seemed interested in only one thing. He grabbed the tin of ginger and carried it back to the man in the other room.

"There. You see," he said, removing the lid. "It's . . . gone!" The color drained from his face.

"It must have been the woman," said the man from Black Mary's Hole.

"No, no, it was there this morning," said the Governor. "I checked. I was feeling rather dizzy and needed a piece of ginger to revive me. It was still there when I looked."

"The boy, then," said the stranger. "He must have found it and escaped!"

"Cirrus Flux?" said the Governor. "But that is impossible! I fail to see how that could be . . ." But his voice faltered and his face fell, dejected.

"There was a girl," said the stranger suddenly, and Cirrus felt his blood go cold.

The Governor looked puzzled. "A girl?" he said. "What girl? There was no one here besides Madame Orrery."

"The girl who climbed over the wall of the hospital," continued the stranger. "I was watching from a distance. Madame Orrery later took her away."

"There was no girl!" insisted Mr. Chalfont, but the other man was already heading for the door.

"Where are you going?" asked the Governor.

"To find the girl and see what she knows. There is a chance she may be involved."

"And what shall I do?" asked Mr. Chalfont, hanging back.

"Keep looking for the boy. And, if you find him, be sure to take back the sphere. It is not safe to keep it here in London. Not with Madame Orrery looking for it—and possibly the Guild."

Mr. Chalfont muttered something under his breath and then hurried after him, racing down the stairs.

Behind the door, Cirrus sank to the floor. His mind was reeling. What was so important about the sphere? Why was everyone looking for it?

The Governor was obviously not to be trusted; he seemed all too willing to hand over the token to the man from Black Mary's Hole. And who was to say that Mrs. Kickshaw, outside looking for him now, would not want it, too?

Perhaps the girl could help him?

He jumped to his feet. There was only one thing to do: he had to get away. He wasn't safe here anymore.

Looping the token round his neck, he tucked it securely under his nightshirt and made his way to the door. Checking to make sure that the coast was clear, he tiptoed down the stairs. He still held the girl's keys in his hand, but didn't want to return to the dormitory in case the boys asked him any unnecessary questions. He would have to steal some clothes from elsewhere.

The answer hit him. The laundry.

He dashed to the back of the hospital and fled across the yard, wincing as bits of gravel stuck to the soles of his bare feet. Then, making sure that Mrs. Kickshaw was nowhere within sight, he crept to the laundry. He scooped up a handful of clothes and raced to the orchard.

He crouched among the shrubs and plants to put them on. The shirt he had grabbed was much too small, so he decided to make do with his nightshirt, stuffing the ends into a pair of loose-fitting breeches. He had no shoes or stockings. Finally, he shrugged on a jacket and climbed the apple tree near the wall.

He very nearly made it, too.

But then, just as he grabbed the rope and started to descend, he heard Mrs. Kickshaw ringing the bell behind him.

"Mr. Chalfont!" she yelled. "It's Cirrus! He's headed for the fields!"

Instantly, he let go of the rope and jumped down, landing in a patch of prickly grass. He sprinted toward the Gallows Tree and then, reaching the dirt road, swerved sharply toward the city.

Within moments he was lost in a maze of buildings, surrounded by clattering carts and noisy people pushing him in all directions. He looked around in bewilderment and then plunged headlong down an alley.

He checked behind him. There was no sign that the Governor or the man from Black Mary's Hole had followed. He had made it. He was free!

❧ 12 ❧

The Face at the Window

Pandora awoke with a start. Where was she? What had happened? The last she remembered she was staring deep into Madame Orrery's eyes, falling into a strange dreamless slumber.

She sat up and looked around, relieved to find her thoughts slowly coming back to her. She was in her room, at the top of the house in Midas Row. The sun was low in the sky and seeds of shadow were sprouting along the walls. What time was it? How long had she been asleep?

She listened carefully. Below her the house was quiet. There were no cries coming from the Crisis Room, no sound of Mr. Sorrel playing the glass harmonica. She tiptoed to the door and tried the handle.

It was locked.

A tray had been placed on the floor inside and she took a

sip of water, desperate to slake her thirst. Immediately, bubbles erupted on her tongue and she spat it out.

She took a closer look at the liquid.

Was this the medicated water Mr. Sorrel used to revive Madame Orrery's patients? If so, had she been mesmerized as well?

Worrying suddenly that Madame Orrery might have seen into her mind, she returned to her bed and lay down, struggling to remember the events of the night before.

Moments later, footsteps padded to the door and Mr. Sorrel looked in.

"What happened?" asked Pandora, turning toward him. "How did I get here?"

"Madame Orrery caught you in the Foundling Hospital," he said angrily. "She brought you back last night. She is most displeased. Whatever were you thinking, child?"

All of a sudden she remembered the curly-haired boy and recalled leaving him in a closet.

"Cirrus Flux," she said. "Is he safe?"

"Madame Orrery says you helped him escape," said Mr. Sorrel disapprovingly. "Do you know where he is?"

Pandora was about to reply, when she noticed Mr. Sorrel giving her a searching look, as though he suspected her of something, and she shook her head, not certain whether she could trust him.

"I do not remember," she lied.

Mr. Sorrel frowned and stared at the floor.

Pandora looked around her—at the scabby walls, the empty grate and the grimy window that opened only a few inches. . . . She was effectively a prisoner.

"What is going to happen to me?" she asked, fearful of what Madame Orrery might do to punish her.

Mr. Sorrel fussed at his sleeves. "I honestly do not know," he said, refusing to meet her eye. "Madame Orrery says you are to remain up here indefinitely. I ought not to be speaking to you now."

He craned his neck to check the door and then said in an urgent whisper, "Please, Pandora, it is not wise to disobey her. If you are not careful, she will take away your thoughts for good. You are fortunate she has not already done so."

"Why hasn't she?"

"Because she believes you may be of some use to her yet," he said. "She's going to use you to help her find the boy."

"Find the boy?" she repeated weakly.

But before she could hear his answer, a bell rang from downstairs and Mr. Sorrel scurried to the door. "Please, Pandora," he said one last time. "Consider what I have told you. Do not cross Madame Orrery again."

With that, he left the room and locked the door behind him.

Dejected, Pandora glanced at the window, wondering how she could possibly get away. From across the city came the sound of church bells tolling, and she counted each long hour as it passed.

Dusk seeped into the room.

Then, just as she was about to close her eyes, she noticed a red flicker against the window.

Instantly, she turned toward it, fearing there was a fire, and let out a startled shriek. A man's face was peering in! He was standing in some kind of wicker basket and hovering in the air.

Pandora leapt back and clutched her pillow to her chest, unable to believe her eyes. Her heart knocked violently against her ribs.

The man tapped on the glass. "*Pssst!* Girl! I need your help!" She could just make out his voice.

Terrified, she turned to the door and wondered if she should call out, but the thought of summoning Madame Orrery filled her equally with dread.

She glanced again at the window.

The man was still there, beckoning her toward him.

Curiosity took over. She peeled herself away from the bed and inched closer, peering nervously into the gloom. A copper moon floated above the man's head. A sail of fabric.

And then she ducked in fright. A fiery creature was flapping its wings beneath the sail, sending plumes of flame into the air.

It was some kind of magical bird!

The man was signaling for her to open the window. Slowly, very timidly, she climbed onto the chest and opened the glass as far as it would go, one or two inches at best. Once again her eyes traveled up to the fierce creature, which whooshed into flame.

"I need to find a boy," said the man urgently, fighting to maintain control of his craft, which thumped against the side of the building. "Cirrus Flux. Do you know him?"

At the sound of the name she went cold.

She shook her head, unable to speak.

The man must have read the expression on her face. "But you know the boy of whom I speak?" he said.

She remained silent.

"Please!" he said. "It's imperative that I find him. It is not safe for him to be alone—not with Madame Orrery looking for him."

Finally, she found her voice.

"Who are you?" she said. "Why should I trust you?"

The man thought for a moment and then took something from round his neck. He held it against the glass.

Pandora peered closer, studying it by the light of the bird. It was a little brass disk, embossed with a lamb. There was a low number on it, too: 016. Her heart started beating faster. If the man was a foundling, he was one of the first!

Suddenly, footsteps sounded on the landing and Pandora turned toward the door.

"Quick! Get back to your bed!" the man instructed her.

Instantly, she obeyed.

Moments later, a key turned in the lock and Madame Orrery looked in. She was carrying a candle. Her eyes flitted from Pandora to the window, which was still slightly open.

149

Pandora whirled round, but the man had gone, vanished into thin air. She was staring at an empty pane of glass.

Madame Orrery looked at her suspiciously. "Trying to escape?" she said, but then seemed to shake the idea from her mind. "Why, it would be a most unpleasant fall. The street is a long, long way below."

She moved into the room and locked the door behind her.

"You really are a meddlesome girl," she said, advancing toward Pandora and placing the candle on the floor beside the bed. "It appears you were telling the truth, after all. The boy, Cirrus Flux, has disappeared. The Governor cannot find him anywhere."

Pandora's heart was racing. She was aware of Madame Orrery reaching into her gown for the silver timepiece.

"What are you going to do with me?" she asked. "How long am I to remain up here?"

"For as long as I desire it," said Madame Orrery. "You could stay here forever and no one would know. Or care."

Pandora delved in her pocket for the scrap of fabric she carried with her, hoping to calm her nerves, but Madame Orrery caught the sudden movement.

"What have you got there?" she asked, and snatched it from her.

Before Pandora could prevent her, Madame Orrery had turned it over in her hands and seen the embroidered letters.

"*Hope.*" She read the word aloud and sneered. "How touching." And then she thought for a moment. "Is this one of those children's tokens?"

Helplessly, Pandora nodded.

A gleam entered Madame Orrery's eye and she quickly bent down to pick up the candle. She held the piece of fabric above the flame.

Pandora leapt back, as if burned. "Don't!" she cried, but Madame Orrery fought off her attempts to get it back and Pandora watched, horrified, as a small brown singe mark appeared on the cloth. An unpleasant odor scorched the air.

"Don't!" she cried again, with an enormous sob, expecting the fabric at any moment to go up in flame. "Please! I'll do anything you ask, I promise! Just don't destroy my token. It belonged to my mother."

A smile curved on the woman's lips. "Good," she said. "I am pleased to hear it." She removed the cloth from the flame and hid it on her person. "You will start by helping me find the boy."

Pandora regarded her with red, swollen eyes.

"How?" she said miserably. "How can I?"

"Tomorrow, we shall visit the man with the all-seeing eye," replied Madame Orrery coolly. "Mr. Sidereal has lenses all over London. There is nowhere for the boy to hide."

❧ 13 ❧

Cirrus, Alone

Cirrus rolled over on the hard, lumpy ground and wiped the sleep from his eyes. He was lying in a churchyard. Gravestones pitted the darkness around him and a tall steeple blocked out the sky.

He sat up. A light was growing steadily bigger and brighter in the adjoining lane.

"Oi! You there!" shouted a watchman, holding up a lantern. "This ground is no place for the living. Off with ye, boy!"

Cirrus staggered to his feet. The night had seeped into his bones and he was shivering with cold. His jacket and breeches were filthy. He moved stiffly away from the churchyard, onto the road.

The watchman shoved him rudely on with his cudgel.

Even now, in the middle of the night, Cirrus was aware of other people shuffling beside him in the dark. Night-soil men removed cartloads of excrement from the yards of the houses, while boys with sputtering torches lounged in doorways, waiting for people to escort home. A church bell tolled the ungodly hour.

Cirrus stumbled blindly on. He had no idea where he was going. His only friend in the world was Bottle Top, but he could no longer remember the name of the gentleman who had apprenticed him or the location of his museum. And he had no way of finding the girl.

He had long since given up asking for assistance. "Out of my sight, boy!" and "Confound your stupid questions!" were just two of the replies he had received from passing strangers the day before. Several times he had even been given a clap on the ear for no reason at all. Finally, exhausted, he had fallen asleep in a churchyard not far from the river.

And now here he was, on the march again.

As soon as he could, he gave the night watchman the slip and disappeared down a side alley. The dome of St. Paul's, which he had been using to navigate his way, was no longer visible, hidden behind a warren of tall buildings.

He kept going.

Gradually, the darkness lifted and people began to file through the streets. Carts and carriages clattered everywhere. So many people. How could he possibly hope to find Bottle Top or the girl in this crowd?

Eventually, he sat down in a sheltered courtyard to rest his weary feet. His head was aching and his stomach panged with hunger. Grocers and merchants were plying their trade in the surrounding streets. He took out his sphere, wishing again that it could show him the right way to go, but all it seemed to do was point at the other side of the world. How had his father come by it? What was it for?

He must have drifted off to sleep, for when he next looked up a gang of boys had crowded round him. Their faces were lean and hungry, and there was a dangerous glint in their eyes.

Cirrus jumped to his feet, but they immediately knocked him down again.

" 'Ere, what's that round 'is neck?" asked the boy nearest him. His coat was riddled with holes, and a sooty neckerchief was knotted round his throat.

"A jewel of some sort," said one.

"A locket, I think," said another.

The first boy, obviously the leader, took a step closer. Cirrus could see a livid scar across his cheek.

The boy caught him staring. "I'm Cut Throat Charlie," he said. "This 'ere's Glass Eye, that's Half Thumb, and over there is Nell. Now, don't be affrighted. We ain't gonna hurt ye. All we want is that sphere."

A hand shot out from beneath the boy's jacket and Cirrus suddenly felt a knife at his throat. He swallowed as its icy edge bit into his skin.

"Move, mind," said Cut Throat Charlie, "and my knife'll slip and take off your ear. Scream"—and his voice was now as sharp as his blade—"and I'll rob you of your tongue."

Cirrus was breathing hard, his heart pounding. He looked

from one boy to the other, wondering if he could escape, but the other boys all looked keen for a fight. They had boxed him in, keeping him out of sight of passersby. The one called Glass Eye was built like an ox, and the boy next to him, though small, had a devious squint. And Nell . . . Cirrus only now realized that she was a girl. A strong, fierce-looking girl with a mop of black hair.

His eyes shifted back to the smaller boy, who held up his hand, a fingerless stump.

Cirrus gulped and was about to plead for mercy when there was a sudden crash from the neighboring road. A horse whinnied, someone shrieked and a thunderous explosion shook the air.

Cut Throat Charlie turned to see what had caused the commotion and Cirrus darted to his feet. He slid out from beneath the blade, which glanced across his cheek, and then dodged sharply as Glass Eye aimed a mistimed blow at his head. The boy's fist connected with Half Thumb instead, who went reeling into the path of Nell.

Cirrus had no time to think. He dashed out of the courtyard and into the street. A cart had collided with a grocer's stall; Cirrus leapt over the carnage and made a hasty retreat.

A cry rose up from behind him.

"Stop! Thief!"

Horrified, he turned to see that his would-be attackers had raised the alarm and were racing after him. They were getting nearer. People were suddenly reaching out for him from all directions, trying to hold him back.

"It's not me!" he cried. "I'm innocent!" But no one seemed to listen and he had to duck and weave to avoid their clutches.

Desperately, he sprinted to the end of the street and raced blindly round the corner . . . right into the path of an oncoming carriage.

As the horse reared above him, Cirrus dropped to the ground and rolled clear under its belly. The horse's hooves came crashing down just inches from his head.

He glanced back. His pursuers were now blocked by the horse and driver, who was unleashing his fury at anyone who came near, lashing at them with his whip. Heart pounding, Cirrus charged up the adjoining street. His lungs were on fire and a great gash of pain was tearing across his side, making it difficult to breathe.

There! Up ahead! He spotted a thin alley between two tottering buildings and raced toward it, forcing himself into the narrow gap, just as another horse and carriage clattered by.

A sour, gassy smell rose from the ground and he cupped his hands over his nose and mouth as he waded further into the gully. Something wet and furry slithered across his foot and he shrank back, disgusted. Still he did not stop until he was well out of sight of the road. He pressed himself against the wall. The buildings were so close together here they almost touched.

He waited. Slime trickled down the wall and oozed beneath the collar of his jacket.

Finally, after what seemed like ages, he began to relax. He could hear nothing of Cut Throat Charlie and decided to follow the passage through to its other end.

Minutes later, he emerged in another street, almost identical to the one he had left behind. He looked around nervously, ready to bolt the instant he saw an unfriendly face, but the shopkeepers were all too busy with customers to notice a wretched waif. He was covered from head to toe in filth.

Further down the street he spotted a large open area. A warm, savory aroma filled his nose and he limped toward it. His ankle was throbbing painfully and he had cuts on his feet.

The market was bustling with people and he searched it hungrily, trying to detect the source of the smell. On a low wooden platform near him stood a man with his head and hands slung through some holes in a post. His body had been pelted with rancid tomatoes. Children were picking whatever edible scraps they could find from the ground.

The smell of gravy tugged at his nose. He turned. A woman with scabby cheeks was selling Bow Wow Pies from a stall.

He moved closer.

All of a sudden a musical voice lifted above the crowd.

"Fireball over London! Earthquake in Devon! Parishioners fall down on their knees and pray!"

Cirrus was sure he recognized the voice. He searched the square and then blinked in amazement as he saw Jonas standing on the opposite street corner, calling out to passersby. He was weighed down with ballads and broadsheets, and was sporting a fresh black eye.

Cirrus rushed over to him.

"Well, I'll be," said Jonas, catching sight of him. "I never expected to see the likes of you again." Then he took another look at Cirrus and shook his head. "What's happened to you, Flux? Run away?"

Cirrus was unsure what to say. Luckily, his stomach chose to intervene. It rumbled loudly.

Jonas heard it, too. "When did you last eat?" he said.

Cirrus shrugged. He had lost all sense of time. He felt dizzy with exhaustion.

Jonas looked around the square. "Wait here," he said, stacking his ballads on the ground, and slipped through the throng.

He returned moments later with two pies.

"Here, sink your teeth into this," he said, handing Cirrus one of them. "Can't tell you what's in 'em, but they're a darn sight better than Mrs. Kickshaw's grub, I daresay."

Cirrus bit into his pie greedily, scooping up every last dribble of gravy with the spoon of his thumb and sucking the crumbs from his fingers long after the pie had disappeared. It was mostly crust and gristle, with a few stringy bits of meat mixed in, but his belly purred with satisfaction.

"Now tell me what's happened," said Jonas, suddenly serious.

Cirrus looked away. He considered telling Jonas everything about the sphere, but then remembered how Jonas had teased him about what he and Bottle Top had seen in the Gallows Tree. He doubted Jonas would believe him.

Jonas was regarding him curiously. "Look. I don't know what made you run away," he said, "but, if you want my opinion, you'd best go back. Life outside the hospital is hard. I've got a good master, but not everyone is so lucky. Trust me. The Governor always liked you. He'll take you back."

Something stirred inside Cirrus—a bitter, resentful feeling—as he remembered how Mr. Chalfont had agreed to hand over his sphere to the man from Black Mary's Hole.

"No, I can't go back," he said firmly. "I need to find Bottle Top. Can you tell me where he is?"

Jonas remained silent and thoughtful for a while, then jumped to his feet. "I can do better than that," he said, dusting off his breeches and collecting his things. "I'll take you there myself."

❖ 14 ❖

The Scioptric Eye

For the second time in as many days Pandora found herself in a horse and carriage. Only this time she was not crouched on the back, clinging on, but was squeezed next to Madame Orrery in the richly upholstered compartment.

She felt like a prisoner in the hot, airless cell. The streets were thick with traffic and carts kicked up dust all around them. A confusion of cries tugged at her ears.

Beside her, Madame Orrery sat still and statuesque, a fan pressed to her nose. This close up Pandora could see fine cracks in the woman's face-paint and faint tea-colored stains under the arms of her dress. She remembered what Mr. Sorrel had told her—how Madame Orrery had once been the most admired woman in France, until her husband had broken her heart—but any sympathy she might have felt immediately evaporated when she recalled how the woman had threatened to burn her mother's token the night before.

160

The carriage rocked and juddered as it passed through the crowds and Pandora scanned the faces that lined the roads, hoping for a glimpse of the boy. She didn't really expect to see him in this moving mass, but she wanted to know that he was safe.

Could the man with the all-seeing eye really find him?

Wharves and warehouses flanked the river to her right, and boats and barges were just visible on the water. Men rolled barrels back and forth along the quays. She thought of the man who had briefly appeared outside her window and wondered again who he was. How did he know Cirrus Flux? And how was he able to hover above the ground?

They continued east, toward St. Paul's.

At last they came to a halt outside an impressive stone building in the heart of the city. It looked more like a temple than a house. Thick columns supported a massive pediment on which sculpted figures reclined, and the roof was surmounted by a vast structure with long windows and an extremely tall lightning rod.

"Mr. Sidereal's observatory," remarked Madame Orrery, following her gaze. "Where he keeps his Scioptric Eye."

Pandora had no idea what this meant, but she imagined a monstrous individual with an eye in the center of his forehead, and a shiver rippled down her spine.

Madame Orrery grabbed her by the arm and forced her up the steps.

A footman answered the door and escorted them into a corridor with pillars on either side. Peculiar jets of flame flickered in glass spheres attached to brackets along the walls.

"What an unexpected surprise," said a thin, fluty voice from somewhere up ahead.

Pandora could not tell at first where it had come from—it seemed to descend from the heights—but then, as Madame Orrery guided her past a row of metal urns, she realized that it belonged to a tiny figure seated on a thronelike chair at the far end of the hall. His chair, Pandora noticed, was set on wheels.

"Hortense," said the little man as they stepped nearer. He reached out to kiss her hand. "What brings you so far from Midas Row?"

"You must know," said Madame Orrery coldly, withdrawing her hand. "I can feel your Eye on me wherever I go."

The man's lips curled in a smile, but there was no trace of humor in his eyes. His face was smooth and delicate, like a child's, and without a single strand of hair.

"Pleasantries aside," he said, "what is the purpose of your visit?"

"I have a favor to ask."

Mr. Sidereal considered her with his jewel-bright eyes. He was dressed in a robe of exquisite silk and wore a matching peacock-colored turban on his head.

"My Eye," he said after a while, arching his brows and elevating his gaze.

Pandora followed suit and saw an airy dome stretching

overhead. A tier of rounded windows circled its base and light fell in streams through the air.

Madame Orrery nodded. "I trust it still functions in this weather?"

"Of course," said Mr. Sidereal. "The dust may have obscured the heavens, but my sights, as you know, are set elsewhere. I can see all over London."

He was silent for a moment and then began to twist a knob on the arm of his chair, setting in motion a series of cogs and gears that moved the wheels beneath. The chair creaked slowly forward.

"Very well," he said, wheezing slightly. "Follow me."

Pandora felt a tug on her arm.

"Go on, girl. Help the gentleman. Push his chair," said Madame Orrery.

Pandora did as she was told. She found two metal prongs attached to the back of his chair and began to push him toward a staircase that sloped along the insides of the walls. There were no steps—just a gradual incline that spiraled round and round, slowly climbing upward.

The man might be small, Pandora thought, but his chair was certainly heavy. She had to lean forward to keep him going. His back was hunched and thin, propped up by pillows, and his short, spindly legs were stretched out in front of him. She studied the swirl of green and turquoise fabric wrapped round his head, wondering if he kept his special eye underneath.

"And who is the girl you have brought with you?" asked the man as they approached a door at the top of the ramp.

Madame Orrery's face hardened. "She is no one," she said. "An interfering child, nothing more."

Two footmen stood before the door and, at a signal from Mr. Sidereal, they swung it open to reveal a dazzling chamber filled with all manner of equipment. Globes and armillary spheres cluttered the floor, while lofty windows offered panoramic views of the whole of London.

Pandora sucked in her breath. She could see far and wide across the city. To the west was the dome of St. Paul's Cathedral, rising above the dingy streets, while far to the north, obscured by haze, were the fields and hills she knew so well from the hospital. The sight brought a pang to her heart.

Long wooden telescopes had been positioned next to the windows, pointing like cannons in all directions.

Mr. Sidereal took control of his chair and wheeled it toward a low circular table in the center of the room.

"Who is it you wish to find?" he asked.

"A boy," said Madame Orrery.

"What is his name?"

"His name is not important."

A shadow passed over Mr. Sidereal's face. "I fear, Hortense, that it is," he said. "I must know exactly what I am looking for if I am to help you find it."

There was an edge of malice in his voice and Pandora saw Madame Orrery hesitate. The woman bit her lip.

"Very well," she said. "If you must know, his name is Cirrus Flux."

There was a long silence.

"Ah, I see," said Mr. Sidereal. "So Captain Flux had a son, did he? How fascinating!" He leaned forward and examined Madame Orrery more closely. "Tell me, Hortense, what makes you so interested all of a sudden in his *orphan?*"

Pandora shuddered at the chilling way he said this word, as though he wished the boy to be without a father. She looked at Madame Orrery.

"He has something I seek," responded the woman flatly. "I need to locate it."

"The sphere?" asked Mr. Sidereal in a high-pitched wheeze, unable to conceal his excitement.

Madame Orrery turned away and said nothing.

"So the rumors are true?" said Mr. Sidereal, wheeling toward her. "The man went to sea without it? Could it be that after all these years the sphere is actually here in London?"

Madame Orrery remained silent and gazed out over the surrounding buildings.

"We seek, I am sure you are aware, the same thing," she said finally. "Only, I know who has it—and you, Neville, can find him for me."

He looked at her suspiciously. "And what is in it for me?" he said. "Supposing, of course, that I help you . . . Or do you propose to go missing, too, like the boy's father?"

Madame Orrery shook her head. "Do not be a fool. Of

course I shall not disappear. We shall unlock its secrets—together—and discover the true nature of the sphere."

Pandora's heart quickened. Did Madame Orrery mean to suggest that the sphere had a special power?

"How very thoughtful of you," said Mr. Sidereal.

There was no warmth in his voice, but Pandora could tell that he was tempted from the way his fingers gripped the armrests of his chair.

"Cirrus Flux, you say?" he murmured, wheeling back to the table. "Describe him for me."

Madame Orrery turned to Pandora. "The girl had a better look at him than I," she said, with venom.

"Ah yes, the girl," said Mr. Sidereal. "Tell me, child, about this boy I am to search for. What does he look like?"

Pandora glanced at Madame Orrery. "Like—like any other boy," she stammered.

"Do not be obtuse," snapped Madame Orrery, and reached into the bodice of her gown. She withdrew not the silver timepiece, but the charred piece of fabric.

Pandora went cold all over.

"Tell him, child, or I shall see to it that our little bargain is fulfilled."

Pandora's heart faltered. She did not want to betray the boy called Cirrus Flux, but she did not want to lose her treasured token, either. She could feel the heat mounting in the room, making it difficult to breathe.

"Dark curly hair," she found herself saying at last. "Green eyes. About my height."

Unexpectedly, she remembered the freckles that had speckled his nose, but decided to keep this detail to herself.

"And would you recognize him if you saw him?" asked Mr. Sidereal, his eyes bright with desire.

She tried to look away, but suspected there was nothing she could hide from his sharp, prying gaze. She nodded unhappily. "I think so," she said.

"Very well," said Mr. Sidereal. He turned to Madame Orrery. "I shall find the boy for you, with the girl's assistance, but on one condition: we share the prize."

Madame Orrery smiled. "Of course," she said, returning the piece of fabric to her gown. "I would not dream of anything else."

Mr. Sidereal grimaced in reply, then grabbed an assortment of lenses from a nearby table and called out to his footmen, "Mr. Metcalfe, Mr. Taylor, if you please. Adjust the curtains!"

Instantly, the two footmen, who had melted into the shadows, rushed forward and climbed a series of ladders around the room, releasing bolt after bolt of black fabric that unfurled like giant bat wings to cover the windows. The observatory was plunged into darkness.

Pandora stood very still, wondering what was going to happen next, and then gasped as right in front of her, on the circular table, a strange apparition began to glow. A ghostly vision of the city all around them, made, it seemed, from grainy shafts of light.

"How does it work?" she said aloud, thinking it must be some kind of magic.

"Optics," said Mr. Sidereal, moving toward her. "I have lenses mounted all over London. On the Monument, around St. Paul's, not to mention the tallest rooftops and steeples. They gather reflections and I study them from here. I can see into every street and corner of the city. Nothing escapes my Eye."

He handed her a pair of special spectacles with numerous eyepieces fanning out from the sides.

Pandora put them on and stared in amazement as figures appeared among the anthill of spires and buildings on the table. Miniature carriages scuttled back and forth through the crowded streets and tiny people went about their business. The figures were faint and fuzzy, but peering closer, using the different lenses, she could just make out their details. In the corner of one street a haberdasher was sweeping the doorway of his shop, while elsewhere a beggar was holding out a hand to passing strangers. A gang of boys streaked by and a flock of pigeons took to the air, circling the buildings like a cloud of midges. She felt like a bird poised above them here, all-seeing but invisible.

Mr. Sidereal had strapped a similar pair of spectacles to his brow and was already scouring the city for a sign of the boy. Pandora focused her attention on the task at hand. If only she could spot Cirrus first, she thought, she might be able to draw attention away from his location.

It was painstaking work. Slowly, parish by parish, they searched for the missing boy, occasionally following the wrong figure through the maze of twisting alleys. Every now and then Mr. Sidereal paused to call out instructions to his footmen, who brought different parts of the city into focus.

The room was stiflingly hot, and her eyes began to tire from the strain of looking at the dusty image. All around the room small spheres of light flickered on the walls.

Mr. Sidereal noticed her wandering eye. "Electrics," he said, pointing to the jets of flame. "I harness the power of lightning from the sky and store its energy in special vials, using my conductors. They fuel the lamps you see before you."

Madame Orrery, meanwhile, was helping herself to a plate of refreshments in the corner. Pandora could see the exotic crown of an unusual spiky object poking out from a bowl of fruit. A pineapple, Mr. Sidereal had called it. Her mouth felt taut and dry, and she longed for a rest, but she could not abandon her post—not when Cirrus Flux might become visible at any moment.

"Twenty degrees north," Mr. Sidereal called up to one of his footmen, who was perched on a ladder high above them, rotating what appeared to be a giant windlass underneath the roof.

Pandora peered up. She could just make out a pinhole of light pricking through the darkness—the source, it seemed, of the apparition on the table.

169

The image shifted slightly and a new vista came into view. A crowded market full of moving people. They bobbed around like pigeons.

Mr. Sidereal paused to wipe his brow and take a sip of sparkling water.

Pandora studied the scene more carefully. A mob had surrounded a forlorn figure, whom children were pelting with flea-sized vegetables. A woman was selling pies nearby.

Her gaze drifted down to the left-hand corner of the square, where things were quieter. Two boys were seated on the paving stones, deep in conversation.

She leaned forward. One of them was dressed in a plain brown jacket—it could have been a foundling's uniform—and had a mass of wavy hair; the other was holding a collection of broadsheets.

"What is it, child? Have you found him?" said Mr. Sidereal, catching her sudden movement and rushing to her side.

Instantly, Pandora backed away, but not before he had a chance to follow her gaze down toward the table.

"A boy with unruly hair, you say?" he said, peering closer and adjusting a dial on the side of his glasses. Another lens slid into place. "How is he dressed?"

Pandora did not respond. She was grasping the edge of the table with her fingers.

Madame Orrery squeezed in beside her. She, alone, did not have a pair of spectacles. "Answer him, girl!"

Pandora's heart was pounding. Her head was spinning. "I

do not know," she confessed. "When I saw him last he was in a nightshirt."

A blush stole across her cheeks, but Mr. Sidereal did not seem in the least surprised by her remark. Against her will, she took another look at the table.

The two boys had risen to their feet and were leaving the square by the northeast corner. To her horror, she saw that one of them had adjusted his jacket and exposed a long white shirt beneath. It might have been a nightshirt.

"Have you found him?" asked Madame Orrery again, snapping her fan with excitement. "Is he there? Tell me what you see!"

"Out of the way!" said Mr. Sidereal. "The girl must make absolutely certain."

To Pandora's surprise, the woman stepped back and allowed Pandora to continue her inspection. She watched as the two figures worked their way across a busy intersection, full of moving carriages, and continued through a series of tightening lanes toward an unknown destination. Where were they going?

They were still too small for her to make out clearly and kept flitting between buildings, but she was almost certain the boy in the brown jacket was Cirrus Flux.

What should she do? Betray him? Or conceal the truth from Madame Orrery?

She could sense Mr. Sidereal beside her, tracking their every movement.

171

At last, the disheveled figures came to a stop outside an impressive garden. A golden statue stood on a plinth at the center of the square and gravel paths crisscrossed the lawn.

"Is he there?" asked Madame Orrery again. "Can you see him? Is he carrying the sphere?"

"Patience, Hortense," said Mr. Sidereal, holding up his hand and peering at Pandora. "Only the girl can tell us."

Pandora held her breath. She could feel them both waiting for her response. She took another look at the table—the image of the square was firmly imprinted in her mind—and then removed her glasses and wiped her brow.

"No," she said at last. "I am sorry to disappoint you. It is a boy not unlike him, however."

Madame Orrery let out an audible groan and collapsed in a chair, but Mr. Sidereal regarded Pandora suspiciously, as if he didn't quite believe her. He had become quiet and secretive all of a sudden. Once again, he looked at the square in which the two boys were standing and then, as if wearying of the enterprise, he wheeled away from the table and clapped his hands. "Mr. Taylor, Mr. Metcalfe!" he called. "The curtains!"

The two footmen immediately swept back the swags of black material from the windows and light flooded into the room. Pandora had to blink away the tears that rushed to her eyes and she watched blurrily as the image on the table slowly dissolved and disappeared.

"Perhaps we shall have more luck tomorrow," said Mr. Sidereal.

Pandora looked out through the tall, laddering windows at the surrounding city. The sky was full of turbulent clouds and had a strange brownish hue, like powdered rust. Thunder rumbled in the air.

And then something caught her eye. A dull copper light rising above the fields, not far from the Foundling Hospital.

Mr. Sidereal saw it, too.

"Ho-ho, what is this?" he said, steering himself toward a telescope that looked out through the north-facing window. "A fireball?"

Madame Orrery jumped to her feet and joined him.

"Oh, this is most remarkable," said Mr. Sidereal, fixing his eye to the telescope and aiming it at the moving target. "It appears to be a flying contraption!"

Pandora did not need a special lens to know what it was. It was the man from last night. He was sailing across the sky!

She stepped away from the window.

Mr. Sidereal continued his inspection. "It appears, Hortense, that we are not alone in our search for the missing boy," he said. "Our old friend the seaman is back in London. Apparently he has contrived an ingenious means of flight—most incredible—and is scouring the streets for him, too. How very, very interesting!"

They were silent for a while, watching as the man drifted over the walls of the hospital and passed across the city, half hidden by the clouds of dust and smoke.

And then, with a growing sense of alarm, Pandora

173

realized where he was headed. She felt Madame Orrery beside her stiffen.

"Why, Hortense," said Mr. Sidereal, as the flying contraption moved steadily over an area of affluent houses and circled a small white church, "I believe you have a visitor."

❦ 15 ❧

The Hall of Wonders

Cirrus reached the southwest corner of Leicester Fields and came to an abrupt stop. Before him was a vast garden, interspersed with gravel paths and planted throughout with small trees. An enormous statue stood on a plinth where the paths converged: a magnificent horse and rider, made, it seemed, from pure gold.

"See what I mean?" said Jonas, beside him. "Fancy, ain't it?"

Cirrus nodded. He was gazing up at the tall white houses that bordered the luxurious square. "Which of 'em is the museum?" he asked.

Jonas pointed to a property on the north side of the square—a palatial residence surrounded by iron palings, with a tiny courtyard set back from the road. Cirrus sucked in his breath. Was Bottle Top really there? In that opulent mansion?

"Are you coming, then?" said Jonas, leading the way.

Cirrus hesitated. Now that he was nearing his destination, he was beginning to lose his nerve. He felt small and insignificant compared to the houses around him and glanced uneasily at his clothes. His jacket was torn and filthy; his legs were covered in slime. Suddenly Jonas grasped him by the elbow and pulled him across the road. A small handbill had been posted outside the museum.

"Look here," he said.

Cirrus stared at the printed notice. He couldn't make out many of the words, but he knew they must be important from the way they were written in impressive letters:

HALL OF WONDERS

TO BE SEEN IN LEICESTER FIELDS

PHILOSOPHICAL FIREWORKS

BEHOLD THE WONDER
AND MYSTERY OF ELECTRICS

FEATURING MR. LEECHCRAFT AND HIS

BEATIFIED BOYS

& FOR THE FIRST TIME

CUPID WITH THE SPARKLING KISS!

MORNINGS & AFTERNOONS WITH AN
EVENING PERFORMANCE   FROM 2S. 6D.

HALL OF WONDERS

Jonas read the sign aloud. "Seems like Mr. Leechcraft's a bit of a swell in these parts," he said, once he had finished.

Cirrus said nothing. His heart had caved inside him. He turned out his pockets. "Have you any money?" he asked Jonas finally.

Jonas shook his head. "Not enough for a ticket, no, if that's what you're thinking," he said. "You're on your own there, I'm afraid."

Cirrus glanced at the door of the museum, which was brilliantly lacquered and ornamented with bright gold.

"P'rhaps you should try ringing the bell?" suggested Jonas.

Cirrus shook his head. His fingers would only tarnish the bellpull, he thought wearily. He backed away from the museum and scanned the rows of windows, wondering what to do. The air was hot and dusty. Thunder rumbled overhead.

"Well, I'd best be off," said Jonas, after a while. "My master will skin me alive if I don't sell a few of these broadsheets before dark."

He patted Cirrus on the shoulder and trotted off across the square. "Good luck, Cirrus," he called out after him.

Cirrus watched him go and then slumped against the garden gate, exhausted. All at once, his tiredness and wretchedness got the better of him and he rested his head in his hands. Fortunately, there were few people around to notice. A maid was dimly visible, polishing the upper windows of a house, and two footmen were attending to a horse and carriage nearby.

Idly, Cirrus fingered the sphere round his neck, wondering

what it was for. Why were so many people after it? He thought of the girl who had come to warn him. What had happened to her?

Some of the countries on the globe didn't quite line up—their coastlines bent and snagged along the equator—and he was just about to twist the halves together when he spotted a gentleman rounding the corner of the square in the company of a small boy. The gentleman was unmistakably the philosopher who had visited the hospital a few weeks before. He was wearing the same purple frock coat and swinging an amber cane. Cirrus did not recognize the boy.

He staggered to his feet.

"Begging your pardon, sir," he said, intercepting them as they headed toward the museum, "but—"

Immediately, the man raised his cane and swept it through the air.

"Out of my way, boy, lest you wish to incur the wrath of my stick!"

"Please, sir," said Cirrus, taking a step back, as the cane narrowly missed his ear. "I don't mean you no harm. I'm looking for my friend is all."

"Cirrus?" a voice piped up beside him.

Cirrus spun round.

The boy was roughly the same size as Bottle Top, but dressed in a lily-white jacket with pearl buttons, silk breeches and silver-buckled shoes. A plump wig nestled on his head.

"Bottle Top?" asked Cirrus, unable to believe his eyes. "Is that you?"

Bottle Top smiled—a smile, Cirrus noticed, filled with other people's teeth. They were gleaming white and new.

"Do you know this waif?" asked Mr. Leechcraft, stepping in between them.

Cirrus saw Bottle Top hesitate and drag his foot across the ground. " 'E's my friend, sir," said Bottle Top softly, without looking up.

"Well, kindly tell your friend to make himself scarce," said Mr. Leechcraft. "He is soiling my doorstep."

"Please, sir, I got nowhere else to go," said Cirrus.

"Is that so? Well, I can count plenty of other places for you to be," said the gentleman. "The workhouse, the jail and the gallows are chief among them. Now, out of my way, boy, before I call the magistrate!"

"Please, sir," said Cirrus. "Allow me to speak to Bottle Top—Abraham—awhile. I need his help."

"Ho-ho!" said Mr. Leechcraft, without much mirth. "And what do you expect my young charge to do? Provide you with employment?"

Cirrus looked at Bottle Top, who had averted his eyes.

"No, sir, but—"

"No buts here, boy. There are to be no charity cases in my presence, do you understand? If you wish to partake of the manifold mysteries of the Hall of Wonders, I beg you to return during opening hours and pay the full admission. If you cannot, then I have nothing more to say to you. Good day!"

He began to move away.

"Please, sir—" said Cirrus, reaching for his arm.

"I said, be off!" snapped Mr. Leechcraft, batting him aside with his cane.

Suddenly another voice spoke up.

"I'll pay," said Bottle Top unexpectedly.

Both Mr. Leechcraft and Cirrus turned round.

"I'll pay," said Bottle Top again, more confidently this time. He reached into the pocket of his waistcoat and withdrew a silver coin. "It's all I got, Mr. Leechcraft, but he's my friend, sir. Only let him stay awhile. Please. 'E ain't no trouble, really."

Cirrus stared at Bottle Top in astonishment, wondering where he had got the money. Mr. Leechcraft, however, scooped the coin into his fist and pocketed it for himself.

"Hmm," he said, considering Cirrus under heavy eyebrows. Finally, he prodded the boy on the chest with his cane. "A foundling, are you?"

"Yes, sir," said Cirrus, unwilling to meet his gaze.

"Run away, did you?"

"Yes, sir."

"Speak up, boy. I can hardly hear you."

"Yes, sir!" said Cirrus, almost shouting the words.

"And why, pray, did you run away?" asked Mr. Leechcraft.

Cirrus ransacked his thoughts for an explanation, but couldn't find one. He glanced at Bottle Top, who was looking concerned.

"I weren't wanted is all," he said eventually, touching the buttons of his grubby jacket, each of which was embossed with the hospital's insignia of a lamb.

"And pray tell me," said Mr. Leechcraft, "does anyone know where you are?"

"No, sir," said Cirrus, and then thought back to his escape from the hospital. Very discreetly, he tapped the token under his nightshirt to make sure it was safely hidden. "At least, I don't think so, sir," he added.

"Hmm," said Mr. Leechcraft again. He scratched his chin. "I reckon the Governor will be mighty interested to learn of your whereabouts," he said at last. "Might even pay a reward for your return, I wager."

"No, sir," said Cirrus quickly, remembering how Mr. Chalfont had conspired with the man from Black Mary's Hole. "Please don't tell Mr. Chalfont, sir. Let me work for you instead."

"Work for me?" said Mr. Leechcraft, aghast. "And what use is a bedraggled boy to me?"

"Please, sir," said Cirrus, rubbing some of the mud from his shins. "There's plenty I can do." He thought of all the things he had been taught to do at the hospital—chores that had seemed so tedious, routine and dull. "I can sew and clean and garden," he said, listing them off on his hands. "I know some words and numbers, even. I can recite whole passages from the Bible—"

"And do you suppose I have need of the Bible?" asked Mr. Leechcraft.

"Yes, sir . . . I mean, no, sir . . . I mean, I dunno, sir," said Cirrus, suspecting a trick in the question.

Bottle Top now took up his cause. "Please, sir. Allow

181

Cirrus to stay awhile. He's a hard worker, sir, just like me. 'E can earn his keep, maybe."

"Yes, sir," said Cirrus, brushing some more of the dirt from his skin.

"Hmm," said Mr. Leechcraft yet again. He ran his tongue along the edges of his teeth and glanced over the boy's shoulder at a wealthy-looking gentleman who was passing by in a gilded carriage. His mouth widened in a smile—and then sprang shut like a trap.

"Very well," he said finally, climbing the steps to the museum. "Come inside, if you must, but do not trail any dirt on the floor of my establishment. Otherwise, I shall have you mopping it up with your tongue."

"Yes, sir. Thank you, sir," said Cirrus, skipping up the stone steps behind him. "I promise I won't let you down, sir. I'll do anything you like."

The man's smile returned to his face. "Oh, I have no fear of that," he said.

The large door opened to reveal a hall crammed with curiosities. Strange animals stood on plinths and pedestals, while masks and totem poles leered at Cirrus from the walls. The ceiling, too, was covered with a miscellany of objects: an overturned canoe, a galaxy of starfish and even a long, leathery crocodile, suspended from invisible wires.

"See that?" said Bottle Top, standing beside him. "That's a Greenland bear. There's only a few of them in existence. And that," he added, pointing to a gray wrinkled beast, "that's half an elephant."

"Where's the other half?" asked Cirrus.

"Somewhere in the jungle, I believe, where I shot it," said Mr. Leechcraft, lowering his face to the young boy's ear and grinning like the crocodile above his head.

Cirrus caught a whiff of the man's bad breath and took a step back, noticing also that Mr. Leechcraft's tongue had a very fine black point to it—as though he had dipped it in poison.

"Now then, Abraham," said Mr. Leechcraft, "kindly see to it that our newest boy is properly attired. Any old outfit should do—Ezra's perhaps—and then show him the museum. Tomorrow, we shall put him to work, eh? Show him the ropes."

"Yes, sir," said Bottle Top quickly, hooking Cirrus by the elbow and propelling him up the stairs.

Cirrus pulled him aside as soon as they were out of sight.

"Thank you for coming to my aid," he said, the words rushing out of him. "I don't know what I would've done if you hadn't been there to help."

Bottle Top shrugged. "It's nothing," he said. "You'd've done the same."

Cirrus looked again at his friend—the fancy clothes, the brand-new teeth, the horsehair wig on his head. He looked just like a proper gentleman.

"Where did you get that money?" he asked.

Bottle Top glanced up and down the stairs, then blushed.

"The ladies give it me," he said.

"Give it you? For what?"

Bottle Top hesitated. "For kisses," he said.

"They kiss you?" said Cirrus, scrunching up his nose, appalled. Then he laughed.

Bottle Top blazed with anger. "It ain't funny," he said. "I'm Cupid with the Sparkling Kiss, the highlight of the performance! Just ask Mr. Leechcraft."

Cirrus quickly wiped the smirk off his face. "I'm sorry," he said. "I didn't mean no offense." He spat on his hand and offered it to Bottle Top. "Are we friends?"

Bottle Top frowned at the dirt on Cirrus's hand, but then accepted it in his own. "Friends," he said.

They spotted Mr. Leechcraft coming up the stairs and rushed on to the next levels of the museum. The abundant trophies that decorated the main hall were soon replaced by empty corridors with flaking ceilings. Patches showed where mirrors and paintings had once been displayed. The walls were gray and dingy.

At last they came to a room at the top of the building. It was just like the boys' dormitory in the hospital—only with fewer beds and fewer boys. Four boys, naked from the waist up, were wrestling on a pair of four-poster beds that had been squeezed into the corner. They were all scrawny and thin, but had tough, bitter expressions, as if they were used to fending for themselves. The floor was strewn with clothes.

"This here's Cirrus," said Bottle Top, running through the introductions, "and that's Micah, Daniel, Ezekiel and Job. They're the Beautiful Boys."

"The Beatified Boys, you oaf," said one of the older boys, chucking a pillow at his head.

The boy who had spoken had fine white scars—like gills—on his cheeks.

"Don't mind Micah," said Bottle Top, under his breath. "He's just sore because I'm the new attraction."

"What happened to his cheeks?" asked Cirrus in a whisper, as the other boys resumed their wrestling match.

"An accident, I believe," said Bottle Top. "A halo shattered during one of the performances and cut his face to shreds. He was even uglier before, I'm told."

Cirrus shuddered, wondering exactly what this meant, but then followed his friend to a basin of cold water that had been set on a dilapidated washstand next to the window. He checked his reflection in a mirror on the wall and started scrubbing the worst of the mud from his body.

He felt tired and sore, but also oddly proud of his battle scars. A thin line of blood had formed where Cut Throat Charlie's knife had nicked his skin.

He toweled himself dry with his nightshirt, careful to keep his sphere out of sight of the others, while Bottle Top rummaged around on the floor for some clothes. Finally, he selected an outfit, not as nice as his own, and handed it to Cirrus. The jacket was made from pale blue silk and discolored here and there with ugly brown marks. Were they bloodstains or burns? Cirrus couldn't tell.

"What happened to Ezra?" he asked, as he slid his arms into the sleeves.

Micah looked up from the bed. "Don't you worry about Ezra," he said. "He's gone to a better place." His eyes turned heavenward. "If you know what I mean."

The other boys chuckled and picked at their hair.

"Ezra isn't important," said Bottle Top, grabbing him by the arm. "You're here now." He handed Cirrus some slightly soiled stockings and, as soon as Cirrus was ready, guided him down the stairs.

"Normally, a tour like this costs half a guinea," he said, as he led Cirrus into the first of the museum's many rooms. "But for you I'm willing to make an exception." He grinned, once again displaying his new teeth.

Cirrus followed, eager to see what the Hall of Wonders contained.

Each room was more startling and lavish than the last. Hundreds of glass cases stretched before his eyes, each filled with curious objects. There were thunderstones, bloodstones, serpentines and agates; feather stars, sea fans, sea lilies and corals; scorpions, scarabs and iridescent beetles. Cirrus had never seen so many things in his life. All the treasures in the world seemed to have been collected and exhibited on the shelves.

He touched the token round his neck, wondering if his father might have been a natural philosopher or an explorer. Perhaps he had seen some of these things himself?

At last they came to a dark, musty room near the back of the museum.

"These are devil's toenails," said Bottle Top, pointing to a cabinet full of spiral-shaped fossils, "back from the days when God drowned the world in the Flood. And these," he said, hurrying over to a case full of sharp, flinty objects, "these are Elf Arrows, used for killing deer in the past. At least, that's what Mr. Leechcraft says." He zigzagged across the room. "Now I want to show you where he keeps his heads."

Cirrus was about to follow when he noticed a thick black curtain hanging in the shadows.

"What's behind there?" he asked, surprised by the goose bumps that had erupted on his flesh. A strange smell, much like Mr. Leechcraft's breath, seemed to hover in the air.

Bottle Top hesitated. "That's where Mr. Leechcraft performs his experiments," he said. "You're not to go down there. At least, not yet. He'll show you soon enough."

He pulled Cirrus toward a cabinet full of skulls and frightening masks. "These are my favorites," he said, smiling happily at a row of shrunken heads. "Gruesome, ain't they?"

Cirrus stared at the ugly, scrunched-up faces. Their eyes and mouths had been sewn shut, and barbs and quills had been thrust through their earlobes and noses.

"First they remove the brains with sticks," explained Bottle Top with relish, "and then they dry the skin. They put pebbles in them to keep their shape. . . ."

Cirrus looked at him, surprised. How did he know all this? Once again, he was struck by the transformation in his friend.

"What happened to your teeth?" he asked.

Bottle Top glanced away and touched his lips. His cheeks were fatter than usual and daubed with white powder, which didn't quite hide the bruising underneath.

"Mr. Leechcraft took me to the best tooth surgeon in London," he said finally. "Mr. Crucius Fang."

Cirrus cupped a hand over his mouth. "Did it hurt?"

"Only a little," said Bottle Top bravely. "The worst bit was the blood."

Cirrus listened squeamishly as Bottle Top described in gory detail everything that had happened: how, after loosening the boy's teeth with a hammer and chisel, Mr. Fang had reached in with a pair of rusty pliers and ripped each of them out from the gum.

"There was blood everywhere," said Bottle Top. "Course, it was all worth it in the end." He stopped to consider his reflection in a glass cabinet. "Mr. Leechcraft says I've got the face of an angel . . . and the Virtue to prove it."

Cirrus took another sidelong glance at the curtain, remembering how Mr. Leechcraft had used the word "Virtue" to describe the strange crackling sensation he had been able to extract from Bottle Top's hair. What sort of experiments did he conduct there?

"What about you, Cirrus?" said Bottle Top suddenly. "What brings you to the Hall of Wonders?"

Cirrus looked around, aware of the eyes watching him from the walls: the masks, skulls and shrunken heads. He didn't know what to say. He was afraid of what Mr. Leechcraft might do if he learned about the sphere—especially if it was as important as the man from Black Mary's Hole made out. He wasn't sure if he should confide in Bottle Top.

Instead, he told him about sneaking off to the Gallows Tree and spying on the man from Black Mary's Hole before running away from the hospital. He made it sound like an adventure. He followed this with an account of how he had escaped from Cut Throat Charlie and finally run into Jonas, who had pointed him in the right direction.

"And now you're here," said Bottle Top cheerfully. "Like old times."

Cirrus nodded. "Like old times," he said, though the smile on his face wavered at the edges.

ᗒ 16 ᗕ

The Moon-Sail

Madame Orrery grabbed Pandora by the arm and dragged her up the stairs.

"You deceiving little creature! You interfering child!" she said. "Just look at what you've done! Thanks to you, that wretched boy is missing, and now that vile man is presumably looking for him, too, in that infernal flying contraption of his. Just pray that I find the boy first, child. For, if I do not, you will never leave this room. I shall leave you up here to rot!"

She threw Pandora into her room at the end of the corridor and slammed the door behind her. The key turned in the lock and angry footsteps charged back down the staircase.

Pandora stood where she was, too stunned to move, and then rushed to the window, hoping the man from before might be there to help her. She had resolved on the way back to the house in Midas Row to ask him for assistance—if not to carry her away, then to pass word to the Governor at the hospital that she was in trouble and needed his help. But the sky was full of turbulent clouds and there was no sign of the mysterious stranger.

Her gaze settled once more on the gallant young knight on the church tower opposite, driving the end of his spear into the curled belly of a dragon. How she wished he could protect her! And then she noticed the plain round shield he was holding, a circular mirror, and was reminded of Mr. Sidereal. What had he said? His lenses were positioned on the highest rooftops and steeples, all trained on the streets below . . .

All of a sudden, she could feel his eye on her, watching her from his observatory halfway across the city, and backed away from the window, into the furthest corner of her room. She crawled onto her bed and lay down, covering herself with a thin blanket of shadow.

Below her the house was quiet. She listened to the silence, breathing it in, remembering Madame Orrery's chilling words from the night before: she could remain up here forever and no one would know, no one would care. . . . She scrabbled in her pocket for the piece of fabric she carried with her and then, with a stab of anger, realized that it was no longer there. Madame Orrery had taken it.

She closed her eyes and tried to block out the feelings eating away at her heart.

She must have drifted off to sleep, for when she next opened her eyes she was aware of a red glimmer in the room,

191

like firelight. She leapt to her feet and, this time, rushed straight to the window.

The man in the basket was there, hovering outside. She could make out the fiery bird flapping its wings above his head.

"Did you find him?" she asked eagerly, opening the window as far as it would go. "Cirrus Flux—is he all right?"

The man leaned toward her. "There was no sign of him, child. Do you know where he might be?"

Pandora thought of the two boys she had seen sneaking around the edge of the square with the golden statue—she was certain one of them had been Cirrus—and was about to tell him what she knew, when she heard something move in the depths of the house. It could have been anything: a shifting floorboard, scuffling mice or even Mr. Sorrel, she supposed, venturing as far as he dared. Or had Madame Orrery been suspicious? Had she been waiting for the man to return all along?

She held her breath and listened, trying to isolate different sounds in the darkness. And then it came again. The sound of footsteps on the stairs.

Someone was coming.

"Please! Take me with you," she said at once. "I can help you find him. I think I know where he is."

The man dipped momentarily out of view as a gust of wind blew him to one side and she feared he was going to leave her, but then he pulled on the ropes connecting the wicker basket to the net of fabric and his grimy face reap-peared.

"I can't, child, I can't," he said, as soon as he was able. "Tell me where to find the boy."

Pandora hopped from foot to foot. She was certain now that the person had reached the landing.

"Please," she said again, her eyes widening in terror. "Madame Orrery knows you're looking for the boy. I think she's coming now. You've got to take me with you!"

The words were spilling out of her and she tugged on the window, struggling in vain to lift it. Tears were streaming down her face.

Her desperation seemed to goad the man into action. With a swift glance at the bird above him, he raised a fist in the air.

"Quick! Step back from the window!" he cried, as, moments later, his gloved hand swung through the pane and showered the air with glass.

A holler sounded from the landing outside and footsteps rushed toward the door. Keys slipped and jangled to the floor.

"Here, give me your hand!" said the man to Pandora, as the door burst open and Madame Orrery appeared.

With a savage cry she lunged toward them and scrabbled for a hold on the girl's ankle, just as the man scooped Pandora into the air.

Pandora felt herself pulled through the open window toward the basket, but Madame Orrery caught her foot and refused to let go. Pandora kicked out in alarm. One of her shoes came loose and spiraled all the way to the ground. She looked down. It was a terrifying drop.

"Alerion!" shouted the man, tilting his head toward the bird, which was flapping its wings above them, struggling to keep the vessel in one place. "Up, girl, up!"

The magnificent bird gave a ferocious squawk and sent a plume of flame into the air. Immediately, the basket began to rise and Pandora was lifted free—away from the window and Madame Orrery's grasping hands. The woman shrieked with rage.

For a heart-stopping moment Pandora dangled outside the basket, treading air, supported only by the stranger's arms, which were hooked round her aching armpits. Then, with a sigh of relief, she felt him begin to haul her in. He lifted her up over the edge of the basket and she slipped into a mound of smelly blankets.

She lay perfectly still, struggling to catch her breath, her mouth open, her heart flailing inside her. Wind rushed through the slats of the wicker basket, cooling her brow, and she could hear the ropes creaking and cracking above her. Just how safe was this rickety contraption?

Slowly, tremulously, she got to her feet.

They were high above the city now. Rooftops drifted far below them, like the floor of a craggy sea, while clouds churned overhead, rumbling with distant thunder. A storm ringed the horizon.

The man was standing next to a slender pole in the

center of the craft, shifting his weight from side to side, riding the air currents like waves. He was dressed in a dark blue jacket that, like the rest of him, was covered in grime. On his head he wore a three-cornered hat, and his breeches were made from some kind of dun-colored hide.

Hot gusts of flame emanated from the bird above them, and Pandora peered up at the majestic creature. It was perched on a bar at the top of the pole, underneath the mouth of bulging fabric. It was amazing! She had never seen anything so graceful and yet so wild. Its wings appeared to be ablaze with fire. Every now and then it lost a feather, which fluttered through the air like a red-hot spark, slowly losing its color.

"She must be so strong, to keep us in the air like this."

The man regarded Pandora with a curious expression. "Aye, that she is," he said. "Alerion is a mighty powerful creature. Though it ain't muscle alone that's keeping us aloft. It's the power of the air."

"The air?" asked Pandora, puzzled.

The man nodded. "Hot air rises, see? And that there sail is harnessing the air that rises off the bird. It's like the mainsail of a boat, capturing the wind. That's what's keeping us afloat."

"The moon-sail?" asked Pandora, failing to grasp his meaning. She gazed into the gleaming sail. It appeared to be made of hundreds of bits of fabric, all stitched together and covered with a resinous glaze.

The man considered her again. "Aye, the moon-sail," he said, with a laugh. "That about sums it up."

A sudden gust of wind punched them to one side and the basket dipped unexpectedly, knocking Pandora off her feet. She landed with a thump against the man's woollen jacket. She inhaled its rich, earthy scent: a mixture of woodsmoke, tar and something else. A faraway spice.

She regarded him more closely, wondering where he had come from and how he knew the boy. For the first time she noticed the peculiar markings on his face: a series of loops and whirls and patterned dots, almost hidden beneath the layers of grime. His eyes, however, were kind—a delicate blue, like bird's eggs discovered in a nest.

The man settled her back on her feet.

"Careful now," he said. "Otherwise it'll be girl over-board—and I ain't planning to be rid of you just yet, not now you've decided to tag along. You've got to show me where to find the boy."

Her spirits sank as she looked down at the darkened streets. It was difficult to see anything in the gloom, let alone a square with a golden statue. Canyons of shadow stretched before her eyes and she could just make out the curve of the Thames as it threaded its way through the city.

"About the boy," she admitted feebly, "I'm not entirely certain where he is. When I saw him last he was in a garden. There was a statue of a horse and rider in it."

The man regarded her for a moment and then let out a weary sigh. "Aye, I feared as much," he said. "That could be anywhere, child. I knew it was a mistake to believe you could help me."

He shifted his weight and the vessel turned away from the river, slowly heading north.

"Where are we going?" she asked, suddenly afraid that he planned to take her back to the house in Midas Row.

"To the fields," he said. "A safe place I know. I'll let you down near the Foundling Hospital. The Governor will take you in, I reckon."

"No!" said Pandora quickly. "You mustn't go there. I don't think it's safe."

The man looked at her, confused. "Whatever do you mean?"

She told him about Mr. Sidereal's eye and the things she had seen from his observatory. "Mr. Sidereal saw you flying above the fields," she said. "He and Madame Orrery know you're searching for the boy. They'll almost certainly look for you there again."

The man was silent for a moment, a frown troubling his brow.

"Mr. Sidereal?" he said at last. "Are you certain? A man in a wheeled chair?"

Pandora nodded. "He has lenses all over London. They're aimed at the ground. I think he knows you from somewhere."

"Aye," said the man. "I've met him before." His voice was grim. "It's worse than I feared. The Guild may already be involved. It's even more crucial that I find the boy and his sphere."

The sphere . . . Once again Pandora glanced at the man, curious to know why he was looking for it as well. But before she could ask any questions, he had taken a spyglass from his pocket and was scouring the city. She noticed a small dent in its side.

Finally the scowl on his face lifted and he put the spyglass away.

"You'd best brace yourself," he said to Pandora. "We'll be anchoring soon."

"Anchoring?" she said, peering down. All she could see was a jumble of rooftops and spires. Where could they possibly land?

"Now don't you worry," said the man. "Just grab hold of something—and don't let go. It may be a bit bumpy at first."

Pandora bunched herself into the furthest corner of the basket and shrank into its sides, reaching up to hold on to the ropes above her. She could tell where they were headed: the cathedral was drawing ever nearer, an enormous chalk-white building capped by a spectacular dome.

"St. Paul's?" she murmured weakly.

The man nodded. "Aye. If, as you say, Mr. Sidereal has lenses all over London, directed at the ground, then I suggest we spend the night in the one place he won't be able to see us. Behind the dome."

Pandora felt a tremor pass through her. All of a sudden the basket they were in seemed very small and vulnerable compared to the massive edifice they were approaching. She tightened her grip on the ropes and took a deep breath as the wind nudged them even closer.

"Steady now, Alerion," the man called up to the bird,

which was carrying them over the surrounding streets. And then, on his instruction, the bird folded its wings.

Immediately, the air grew still and quiet, apart from the silken rustle of the sheets. Pandora watched as the moon-sail lost its luster and light.

For a moment the basket continued on its upward trajectory; then, as the air around it cooled, the vessel started to sink.

Slowly at first, then faster.

Pandora felt a slight wobble beneath her feet. The man had fixed his sights on a narrow strip of roof and was steering them toward it—directly between two tall stone towers that flanked either side of the main entrance.

Pandora sucked in her breath. They were coming down too fast! They weren't going to make it. The impact would surely smash them to bits!

But the man showed no sign of trepidation and, just as the basket neared the ledge, he released an anchor from the side of the basket and a length of rope slithered out from behind them. Pandora could hear the metal claws scratching and scraping against the stone as the basket finally landed with a thud and began to judder across the tiles.

For a moment they careened out of control, skidding toward the edge, but finally the anchor sank its teeth into the rooftop and the rope pulled taut with a jerk, overturning the basket.

Pandora was thrown out head over heels, landing with a hard, vicious smack. The world spun before her eyes and her palms felt as if they were on fire—grazed from where she had tried to cushion her fall. She doubled over in pain.

The man was instantly by her side. "Are you hurt?" he asked, easing her into a sitting position. "Answer me, child."

She was dimly aware of Alerion streaking across the sky above them, a red ball of flame.

"Pandora," she managed to gasp, as the first fiery breath forced its way into her lungs. "My name is Pandora."

The man's face broadened into a smile. "I told you not to let go, Pandora!"

Bracing herself on his arm, she managed to hobble back to the moon-sail, which was deflating around them like a sigh. Alerion fluttered down and settled on the rim of the perch, a ready-made fire. Above them rose the dome of the cathedral, blocking out the sky—and, Pandora was relieved to see, that part of the city housing Mr. Sidereal's eye.

She settled herself on the rooftop and stared into the bird's brilliant red and gold plumage, while the man pulled a variety of sacks from the basket.

"Here, eat this," he said, handing her a wedge of a flattened meat pie. "It will make you feel better."

Only now was Pandora aware of the hunger growling in her stomach. She sank her teeth into the cold, greasy pie.

Alerion was watching her intently, with glittering eyes, and then gave a raucous screech—just like the animal cry Pandora had heard the other night in the fields.

"It was you," she said suddenly. "The light I saw—the sound I heard—when I was sneaking into the hospital."

"Aye," said the man, tossing the bird some scraps. "I was watching you the whole time."

He sat down on the other side of the bird and Pandora studied him closely. Shadows flitted across his face. Once again she noticed the strange markings on his skin.

"Who are you?" she said. "And why are you looking for the boy?"

The man was silent for a while. At last he said, "My name is Felix Hardy. James Flux was my friend. He was Cirrus's father. We were foundlings together."

He stared into the bird's flickering feathers. "The truth is, I come back to take something that don't rightfully belong to the boy. That don't rightfully belong to anyone, for that matter . . . The Breath of God."

"The Breath of God?" repeated Pandora, not certain that she had heard correctly. "What is that?"

"A secret substance James discovered on the other side of the world," said Mr. Hardy. "It's contained in a sphere. Like many people, Madame Orrery believes it possesses great power. James was supposed to locate more of it for the Guild of Empirical Science, but . . . he never did."

His voice trailed off and his eyes took on a distant look.

"A sphere?" said Pandora. "You mean Cirrus's token?"

Mr. Hardy eyed her with surprise. "Aye," he said. "Have you seen it?"

"Once," she said. "In the Governor's study. I saw Madame Orrery looking for it later. It wasn't there." Her heart started

201

hammering. She remembered mentioning it to the boy. "Does Cirrus have it now?" she asked. "Did he find it?"

Mr. Hardy scratched his brow. "Aye, I believe so," he said. "It went missing from the hospital the same time he disappeared."

Pandora was quiet for a moment, trying to take this in. "And that's why we must find him now," she said after a while.

The man looked at her again. "Aye," he said. "As soon as the sun's up, we'll start looking for the boy. But for now, Pandora, you must rest."

He rose to his feet and pulled a couple of blankets from the basket. Pandora draped them on the ground and snuggled closer to the bird, whose feathers cast a warm, pleasant glow on her skin.

Her mind was too full of questions, however, to let her settle. "Tell me about the other side of the world," she said. "And how you found this magical bird . . ."

The man made a face, but appeared to relent. "Very well," he said. "Just a few words."

She nodded happily and lay on her back, staring up at the thick, stormy clouds gathering above them.

"It was a long time ago," he said in a husky voice. "James and I had been commissioned to set sail to the edge of the world. We were to find the Breath of God. It was a hard voyage, doomed from the start. Cirrus had just been born, but Arabella—she was Cirrus's mother—died in childbirth. James had no choice but to leave the boy behind."

"At the Foundling Hospital," said Pandora.

"Aye," said Mr. Hardy. "The Governor took him in. James did not know what else to do." The man hesitated for a moment and then picked up the story, further along. "The winds were against us the entire way. We battled seas the likes of which I have never known. It was as though Nature knew the error of our ways. . . ."

Pandora listened, her chest rising and falling to the rhythm of his words, imagining the fearful waves, but by the time the ship reached the tip of Cape Horn she was asleep.

"And then disaster struck," said Mr. Hardy, to himself, taking a swig of brandy from a flask in his pocket. "The ship was caught in the fiercest gale I have ever seen, a storm that took the whole crew down. . . ."

Eleven Years Earlier

OFF CAPE HORN,
1772

An enormous wave rises above the boat and slams down, sweeping the exhausted men off their feet. Water is gushing through a hole in the hull and Felix knows the awful truth: the ship is going down. There is nothing anyone can do to save them.

The wind howls in his ears and rain slashes across his face as he battles his way back to the quarterdeck. A lone figure stands at the helm, steering the stricken boat through the worst of the storm, heading toward a horizon he alone can see—a distant band of ice and fog, blocked by a battlefield of wave and cloud. It is as though the sea and the sky are at war with each other. Waves climb toward heaven and then topple down, while clouds burst overhead, lit by jubilant flashes of fire.

And then, out of the corner of his eye, Felix spots a vicious crag of rocks, a terrifying cliff, rising out of the water.

His blood runs cold and he swallows back the acid taste of fear in his mouth.

He turns to starboard and screams, "James! To starboard! Ahoy!" But the wind strips him of his voice and stretches it to a thin whisper. It is lost in the gale.

Another wave looms, rolling in their direction until it blocks out the sky, which is suddenly as black as night. And then his heart sinks, for he sees it curl at the edge, a lacy trim, and almost before he can brace himself, it hurtles toward the boat, smashing into the hull with the full force of a whale.

The boat buckles and trembles and tumbles to one side, its masts spearing the sea. Yet more men are thrown, shrieking, from the ropes, where they have been desperately trying to mend the shredded sails.

Felix is thrown across the deck and only just manages to hang on to the gunwales.

Slowly, agonizingly, the boat begins to recover and rights itself. The wood groans and water sluices over the side. Felix staggers to his feet, a gash in his forehead reddening his vision. The sea is flecked with bits of wood, and men float, senseless, in the waves, their coats jellyfishing around them. The air is full of drowning cries for help.

Desperately, he works his way back to the helm.

But no one is there.

James—his oldest, truest friend—is gone.

Felix lets out an anguished howl and then, realizing that no one is in command of the sinking ship, grabs the wheel and tries to rectify their course. But it is no good. The ship pitches ever more violently toward the rocks.

And then he hears a terrifying sound. A deep rumble in the bowels of the ship, a thunderous crack that runs all the way up to the top of the mast. A grating, tearing, rasping sound, as though the boards are being prised apart and the nails wrenched away.

Felix looks up and sees the mainmast totter and lean. Before he can raise the alarm, another wave punches him in the face and slams water down his throat.

It is too late. The mast has splintered and, like a great tree falling, it spills over the side of the boat. Ropes fly and whistle, shrilling through the air, and yet more men are hurled to their death.

The sky flashes with fire and the waves rejoice. And still the rain comes sleeting down, hissing like arrows into the sea.

Felix turns. To his right, the enormous ridge of rocks is crashing closer, its jagged teeth shredding the sea to vapor. He has no choice. He crosses himself and plunges into the icy water.

The shock of it is like a hammer blow, forcing all the air out of his chest. For a moment he loses himself in the swirling darkness and then, instinctively, he begins to claw his way back toward the surface.

Choking and retching and gasping with cold, he breaks through, coughing up lungfuls of burning seawater. Salt blurs his eyes. He can just make out the boat nearby, slamming into the rocks. It gives one last excruciating moan and then starts to go under.

Immediately the towrope whips out and snags him, dragging him down by the ankle. The water closes over him. Tired though he is, he struggles against it.

Finally, when he thinks he can hold his breath no longer, the sea relents and he slips from its grasp, kicking once more toward the surface.

The waves lift him in each swell, a crazy cradle. He tries to get his bearings, but all he can see is the boundless water.

No. The torso of a woman floats nearby.

Exhausted, he swims toward it. It is the figurehead of the ship, all that remains of the sunken vessel. With bleeding fingers he clings to it, a drowsy numbness weighing on him like an anchor.

He forces himself to keep moving, treading water, but the cold is crippling. His teeth chatter and his limbs have lost all feeling.

Nevertheless, he can sense the storm abating. The wind is not so strong now; the waves are not so vicious. A spark of hope ignites within him. He can just make out the horizon.

Two flares of light are drifting closer. . . .

What are they? Angels?

They soar across the sky on wings of flame.

But, no, they are too late. The water is closing around him again and he is sinking under. . . .

Just as his mind begins to blur, something dives into the

water. Two sharp hooks grab him by the shoulders and lift him, nearly senseless, from the waves.

He is floating—flying—through the air, though how this is possible he cannot fathom.

Perhaps he is dead. Or merely dying?

A distant heat reaches his body, but it is not enough to wake him. The world folds over and turns black.

When next he opens his eyes, he is lying on a rough, pebbly shore. Waves lap and sigh around him, but they are gentle now, a murmur. His throat is parched and his lips are raw and shriveled. A peaty smell of woodsmoke hovers in the air.

From behind him he can hear the jabber of strange voices and the crackle of a blazing fire. Enormous trees with slender trunks and bushy canopies stand on the periphery of his vision.

Suddenly, there is a patter of feet beside him and he looks up to find a child with long black hair and the most beautiful smile he has ever seen staring down at him. An animal skin has been draped across the child's shoulder, and on this perches a bird of fire.

Felix squints. Yes, it is true. A bird with wings of flame! He wonders if this is what plucked him from the waves.

The child crouches beside him and pours something wonderful and soothing into his mouth. Cool, delicious water. Felix drinks it in and then closes his eyes with a smile.

Everything fades once more to black.

Eleven Years Later

LONDON, 1783

❧ 17 ❧

The Halcyon Bird

The sound of footsteps woke her. Pandora tilted her head to one side and saw the hefty figure of Mr. Hardy approaching. He was dressed in his heavy seafaring jacket, dun-colored breeches and knee-high leather boots. He was carrying something else in his hands, too. Clothes.

He placed them on the ground beside her and strolled over to where the basket still lay after its bumpy landing the night before. From a sack inside, he pulled out a crusty loaf of bread, a slab of cheese and a flask of brandy.

Pandora ran her fingers over the warm, woolly garments. They were simple, hard-wearing clothes: a short bum-freezer jacket, a linen shirt and a pair of loose-fitting trousers, like those any sailor might wear. He had even remembered to include a pair of stout leather shoes.

"Where did you get them?" she asked sleepily.

The man sliced himself a wedge of cheese. "I bought 'em good and proper from a man I know in Dolittle Alley," he said. "Traded one of my best instruments for 'em, too. Now get dressed. We've much to do."

Excited, Pandora scooped up the clothes and carried them over to the side of the dome, where she could change in private.

Above her, on a ledge, pigeons burbled noisily and a sharp wind gusted round the edges of the cathedral. She had to step carefully because the tiles sloped dangerously underfoot and there was a steep drop to her left.

She removed her foundling's dress and tugged the unfamiliar garments over her body. Her skin was covered in plum-colored bruises.

"Thank you," she said, shyly emerging from behind the dome and walking back toward him. "No one will recognize me in these fine clothes."

"That's the idea, child," said Mr. Hardy. "Now put this on your head."

He tossed her a red cap, made from knitted wool, which she pulled over her short auburn curls. She stood before him while he looked her up and down.

"A reasonable fit, all things considered," he said, cutting a length of rope from a coil in the basket. He looped it quickly round her waist and tied the ends in a knot. "Can't have your trousers falling down if you're to be my Able Seaman, can we?"

Pandora blushed, not sure whether it was from embarrassment or pleasure.

"Are we flying again in the moon-sail?" she asked hopefully, her eyes drifting to the net of fabric.

"Course not," said Mr. Hardy. "It ain't safe, child, not with Mr. Sidereal watching." He motioned toward the ground with his knife. "No, we're going to do some walking. Now get some food down you and we'll be off."

He offered her a hunk of bread and cheese, which she followed with a sip of his brandy. The rich, fiery liquid stripped the back of her throat and made her eyes water. She coughed a little and then smiled as a warm sensation glowed in her stomach.

At this moment Alerion swooped down from the top of the belfry and alighted on the metal perch between them. Pandora gazed into the bird's red and gold plumage, marveling at its appearance. Each feather was like a spark, ready to ignite into flame.

"What is she exactly?" she asked, breathless with admiration.

Mr. Hardy reached into a sack behind him and pulled out a dozen dead rats, tied together by their tails. Alerion was watching him closely, her eager eyes aflame. Her short, curved beak opened to reveal a crimson tongue.

"A Halcyon Bird," he said, tossing Alerion a rodent.

She snared it in her claws and pulled strings of meat from the carcass.

"Where did she come from?"

"From the other side of the world," said Mr. Hardy. "Like I told you. An island no bigger than this city, off the tip of Cape Horn."

Pandora peered into the distance—past the wharves and warehouses along the riverbank, and the tanneries and mills. All she could see at the far end of the city was a forest of masts and rigging.

"There was an ancient people on that island," continued Mr. Hardy. "The Oona tribe. They spoke another language. They could even speak to birds."

Pandora's eyes widened. "How, then, did you understand them?"

Mr. Hardy was silent for a moment. "Like all things, it took time," he said. "I learned some of their ways; they learned some of mine."

Alerion was preening herself, fluffing her wings, sending hot sparks into the air. He tossed her another rat.

"They were a peaceful tribe," he said, rising to his feet and walking to the edge of the cathedral. "They belonged to the earth, whereas we"—he swept his eyes over the city—"we believe it belongs to us."

Pandora stood beside him. For an instant the sun broke through the clouds and transformed the river into gold. The city glowed in a luminous haze. But then, just as suddenly, the sun dipped back into hiding and the city was filled again with shadow and smoke.

"You say they *were* a peaceful nation," said Pandora hesitantly. "What happened to them, Mr. Hardy?"

He stared into the distance. The light faded from his eyes.

"The Oona tribe is gone, girl," he said. "Dead."

He marched back to the moon-sail and started shoving supplies into the basket. "After our ship went down, others came looking for the Breath of God. Some chanced upon the island. When they discovered that I did not have the sphere—indeed, that James had not brought it with him—they took whatever they could find and killed the birds for sport."

Mr. Hardy glanced at the bird above them. "Only one egg was spared and that was Alerion's. A Halcyon Bird, see, takes years to hatch. They're resilient creatures, but rare. Alerion . . . well, she's the last of her kind."

Pandora stared at the bird with burning eyes. Tears were running down her cheeks.

Mr. Hardy's voice was now little more than a whisper. "The ships left something even more terrible in their wake. Disease. The whole tribe was ravaged by fever. I was the only survivor. Eventually I flagged down a passing ship, using light reflected from a mirror, and worked my way back to this godforsaken island."

He reached into a sack, pulled out another dead rat and flung it to Alerion, who snagged it in her claws and devoured it.

"She certainly eats a lot," said Pandora, watching carefully.

Mr. Hardy finally managed a smile. "Aye. Halcyon Birds grow at an alarming rate and this one's got a voracious appetite."

"May I feed her?" asked Pandora suddenly.

Mr. Hardy turned toward her. "I don't see as why not," he said, offering her a rat. "Flinging it by the tail is best."

"No," said Pandora nervously. "I mean, may I feed her . . . by hand?"

Mr. Hardy swallowed. "Oh, I don't know about that. She's a mighty fearsome creature. Halcyons don't take kindly to strangers."

"Please," said Pandora. "I'd like to try."

Alerion cocked her head and regarded Pandora with a ruby eye.

"Very well, if you must," said Mr. Hardy, rising to his feet. "But first put on these." He handed her a pair of thick leather gloves. "Otherwise, she'll make a feast of your fingers."

Pandora slid her hands into the scabby interior, as stiff as a plate of armor round her wrists.

"Now raise your arm," said Mr. Hardy, "and hold it steady like the branch of a tree."

Pandora did as she was told, shaking a little as Alerion bobbed up and down. And then, in a blaze of fire, the bird leapt forward and hooked her talons round Pandora's narrow wrist. She settled there, surprisingly light and agile.

A laugh escaped Pandora's lips. She could feel the fiery feathers burning into her skin, but she didn't want to let go; she wanted to hold on to this moment forever. She accepted a rat from Mr. Hardy and, with her spare hand, raised it carefully to the bird's beak, watching as Alerion ripped long fatty ribbons from the gray body.

"She's beautiful," Pandora said, her heart thumping inside her.

"Aye, that she is," said Mr. Hardy fondly. "But now, Pandora, we must go. We've a boy to find."

Pandora carried Alerion back to her perch and then followed Mr. Hardy to the corner of the roof, where a ladder led down to a small door in the nearby bell tower.

"How are we going to find him?" she asked.

"I've been thinking about that," said Mr. Hardy. "You say that Mr. Sidereal's been watching the city from his observatory high above the rooftops. Well, I suggest we start by watching him instead. For, if what you say is true and he may have seen the boy, I reckon it's only a matter of time before he leads us to him."

221

⚜ 18 ⚜

The Hanging Boy

Cirrus was in the aviary when Bottle Top found him.

The Hall of Wonders had closed its doors for the afternoon, allowing the boys a few hours of precious freedom before the evening performance. Cirrus had come here on his own, preferring the company of the birds to the rough-and-tumble boys, who were no doubt still wrestling on the beds upstairs. Hundreds of birds were arranged in the glass cases around him: toucans, peacocks, parrots, owls and even luminescent hummingbirds that dangled from the ceiling.

He climbed one of the ladders that had been propped up around the room and began wiping a rag along the jars.

"What're you doing?" asked Bottle Top, reclining on a cushioned bench behind him. Only a handful of visitors had trickled through the museum that afternoon, but he had regaled nearly all of them with his accounts of the more gruesome exhibits. His voice was hoarse and croaky.

"Mr. Leechcraft told me to make myself useful," said Cirrus, spitting on a jar and buffing it to a fine polish. "I'm cleaning the cages."

"Well, he ain't here now, so you don't have to work so hard," said Bottle Top, removing one of his shoes and massaging his heel.

Cirrus said nothing, but continued wiping his rag along the shelves. Up close, he could see that many of the birds were badly stuffed, fixed with twine or else pinned by rusty nails to the branches that were supposed to represent their natural habitats. Some of their eyes had fallen out, and their bodies were coming undone at the seams.

"Don't you ever feel sorry for these birds?" he said at last. "They ought to be free, not cooped up here in cages."

"They're dead, Cirrus."

"Well, they oughtn't to be," said Cirrus. "It's not right. Things oughtn't to be left to rot like this."

Bottle Top was watching him closely. "What's on your mind, Cirrus? Is there something you ain't telling me?"

Cirrus shook his head. One of the jars was particularly dusty and he blew on it to reveal a small speckled bird inside. It had an ornate feathery headdress and a wide, gaping bill. He read the label—*Owlet Nightjar, Native of Australasia*—and patted the token from his father, resolving to find out later where that was.

"Don't you like it here at the museum?" continued Bottle Top.

"It isn't that," said Cirrus, adjusting the cord round his

neck. "It's just that I wasn't entirely honest yesterday about why I left the hospital."

Bottle Top rose from his bench and drew up another ladder so that he was side by side with his friend. "Tell me," he said.

Cirrus was quiet for a moment, dusting and redusting the same jar, then he finally told Bottle Top about sneaking into the Governor's study and finding the ledger full of names and numbers.

"There were tokens, too," he said. "In the drawers. One for each child, I should reckon. Keepsakes, mementoes and letters full of grief and sadness, written by mothers for the babies they had to leave behind." He took a deep breath. "Only there weren't nothing like that for me."

Bottle Top regarded him thoughtfully. "I don't see why you're so upset," he said eventually. "We was all abandoned at the hospital, Cirrus. Ain't none of us was truly wanted. That's why we're to look after each other now."

"That isn't all," said Cirrus, inching closer to the truth. "I found out who it was left me there." He gripped the sides of the ladder and stared straight ahead. "My father," he said.

"Your father?"

Cirrus felt a chill creep over him. "Turns out he paid to get rid of me."

Bottle Top's jaw dropped open.

"How much did he pay?" he asked in a whisper.

Cirrus continued dusting the owlet nightjar, pretending he had not heard.

"How much?" asked Bottle Top again.

"A hundred pounds," said Cirrus very softly.

Bottle Top's face was suddenly alive with excitement. "A hundred pounds! You know what this means, don't you?" He grabbed Cirrus by the arm. "You're from a wealthy family, Cirrus! Gentry, even! Only a rich gentleman could afford a sum like that."

Cirrus stopped rubbing the glass jar and frowned at his reflection. "It doesn't mean that at all," he said. "It means I weren't wanted. I weren't wanted so much, my father paid to get rid of me. I must have been a great disappointment to him."

"Nonsense," said Bottle Top. "It means you're special, Cirrus! You was always the Governor's favorite for a reason."

Cirrus whipped his hand away and stared at his friend. "What's that supposed to mean?" he said.

"Just what I told you," said Bottle Top. "The Governor always treated you special. Like you was royalty or something."

"Well, you don't know anything," said Cirrus bitterly, and jumped down from the ladder. "Your mam probably dropped you off at the hospital the moment she laid eyes on you."

Cirrus stormed to the other side of the room and climbed another ladder to hide his emotions. He was annoyed with Bottle Top for not sympathizing with his situation, but he was also hurt and angered by his father for abandoning him at the hospital all those years ago. Besides, Bottle Top was wrong: Mr. Chalfont couldn't have cared about him that much; he

225

had been willing to give the man from Black Mary's Hole his token, after all.

Breathing heavily, Cirrus set to work on the remaining jars. Some of them looked as though they hadn't been cleaned in ages, and he flicked his rag at them angrily, expelling little clouds of dust in the air.

Suddenly, he stopped.

One of the jars contained a pile of feathers that looked nearly identical to the ones he had seen below the Gallows Tree only a few weeks before. A heap of light gray ashes, streaked here and there with orange and crimson. He found a label near the bottom of the jar, written in a spidery hand:

Incendiary bird, discovered off the coast of Tierra del Fuego. Possibly related to the phoenix. The bird builds its nest at the top of tall trees and lines it with a special paste to make it impregnable to fire.

Cirrus creased his brow, struggling to make sense of the words, and was just about to check the sphere round his neck, to see where Tierra del Fuego might be, when he caught Bottle Top watching him from the other side of the room.

"What you got there, Cirrus?" asked Bottle Top moodily.

"Nothing," said Cirrus, returning the sphere to its hiding place.

"You're lying. I saw it. There's something round your neck."

Bottle Top got down from his ladder and moved toward him, but then a bell shrilled somewhere in the museum and he turned to the door.

"What's happening?" asked Cirrus, dismounting more slowly.

"It's time for the evening performance," said Bottle Top quickly. "I've got to prepare."

He scurried back through the museum. Silently, Cirrus put down his rag and followed.

Upstairs, the other boys were hurriedly pulling on their jackets and dabbing rouge on their cheeks. The air swam with perfume and powder. Bottle Top was seated before a tarnished mirror on the wall, checking his reflection.

"Pass me that bottle of ceruse, will you?" he demanded, as Cirrus walked past.

Cirrus looked around, found a bottle of smelly white powder and handed it to Bottle Top, who smeared it all over his face.

Cirrus watched him in the glass.

"I'm sorry," he said at last.

"What for?" said Bottle Top, averting his eyes.

"For what I said earlier," said Cirrus. "About your mam. I didn't mean it. I know she would've cared." He hesitated. "As do I."

Bottle Top tilted his face and applied some more powder to the base of his chin. Then he smacked his lips together and opened his mouth.

227

"Doesn't matter," he said finally, inspecting his teeth. "Now pass me my wings."

Cirrus glanced around the room, confused, and then saw a silver jacket with two surprisingly heavy wings, made from goose feathers, protruding from the back of it.

"You look just like an angel," said Cirrus aloud as Bottle Top slid his arms into the sleeves.

Bottle Top took one more look at himself in the mirror and grinned. "I'm Cupid with the Sparkling Kiss," he said.

Another bell rang and the boys promptly grabbed their wigs from the wooden bedposts, where they had impaled them, and tramped down the stairs. Bottle Top followed more slowly, taking care not to damage his wings, while Cirrus lagged a few steps behind.

Two flights down, he noticed that one of the doors was ajar and peeked in to see Mr. Leechcraft seated behind a worn wooden desk. The man's head was wigless and bare, in need of a shave, and he had rolled up his shirtsleeves, which looked grubby and soiled.

Mr. Leechcraft caught him watching and rose from the chair. He took his wig from its stand, grabbed his amber cane and quickly advanced toward the door, donning his frock coat as he came. By the time he reached the landing he was a new man.

"Are you ready, my boy?" he said to Bottle Top, who was waiting nearby.

Bottle Top nodded and a halo of powder drifted down to the ground.

"Good. Perform well tonight," said Mr. Leechcraft, "and there'll be a shilling in it for you. I am expecting a special guest. A gentleman from the Guild."

"The Guild?" asked Cirrus, convinced he had heard the word somewhere before.

Mr. Leechcraft regarded him curiously. "The Guild of Empirical Science," he said, arching a brow. "The foremost body of natural philosophers in the land. Impress upon them the importance of our work here and our fortunes will be assured. I trust you will not let me down, Abraham?"

Bottle Top straightened. "Don't you worry about a thing, sir. I'll make the audience scream!"

"Good," said Mr. Leechcraft, tapping him on the shoulder with his cane. Then he turned to Cirrus and his expression changed. "As for you," he said, running his eyes over the boy's unruly hair, "watch everything closely and keep out of sight. Do I make myself clear? I have not decided what to do with you yet."

"Yes, sir," said Cirrus.

"Now come along. We haven't much time."

Swinging his amber cane, he led the pair down the steps and through the darkening hall, full of shadowy exhibits, to a special auditorium at the back of the museum. Cirrus felt a vague sense of apprehension creep over him as they approached the black curtain he had seen before.

"Welcome to my Electrical Chamber," said Mr. Leechcraft, sweeping the curtain aside. "Where I perform my investigations into Aethereal fire!"

229

They entered a small amphitheater, lit with flickering candles. Tiers of gold-backed chairs surrounded a stage, on which various pieces of equipment had been arranged. Cirrus was immediately struck by a lethal-looking machine with two glass disks, the size of cartwheels, suspended vertically within a tall wooden frame. This was attached to a long metal rod that extended halfway across the stage.

Mr. Leechcraft snatched a candelabrum from a passing boy and led them down the aisle.

"This is my electrostatic machine," he said, stroking the gleaming gun barrel with his hand. "When I turn the handle here"—he indicated a crank behind the glass wheels—"sparks of Aethereal fire rush out of the other end. It is most extraordinary."

Cirrus, however, was momentarily distracted by a flat wooden swing that Micah was lowering from the ceiling. It came to rest just a few inches away from the nose of the machine.

"Ah, the highlight of the performance," said Mr. Leechcraft, looking at Bottle Top expectantly. "The Hanging Boy."

As Cirrus watched, Bottle Top slipped off his shoes and wriggled into position on the swing. He lay lengthwise, so that his chest and stomach were pressed against the board, but his arms and legs were free to dangle from either end. It looked just as if he were swimming in midair.

Mr. Leechcraft adjusted one of the straps round the boy's

waist, binding him to the swing, and then, with a final word of warning—"Remember, Abraham: Mr. Sidereal will be watching and so, my boy, shall I"—stepped back into the shadows and disappeared, leaving the boys alone together on the stage.

Micah sidled up to Bottle Top as soon as Mr. Leechcraft had gone.

"Anything the Leech offers you tonight is mine, got it?" he said, further tightening the straps that bound Bottle Top to the swing.

Bottle Top winced. "Careful! You're hurting me. They're too tight. I can't hardly move or breathe!"

Micah eyed the fragile-looking pulley in the rafters holding everything in place. "That's the idea," he said. "Now keep still and be quiet. And remember who's in charge of the ropes. You don't want to meet with a nasty accident, do you? I'll expect my nightly fee when I let you down."

Bottle Top fell silent and eventually stopped wriggling, as Micah began heaving on the ropes, hoisting him into the air.

Within moments Bottle Top was hanging high above the stage, near the rafters, surrounded by clouds of billowy black material that Cirrus supposed were meant to hide him from view. Sequins glittered on the fabric like stars.

All around him the other boys were making final preparations for the performance. They rolled heavy gray cylinders, the size of milk churns, across the stage and sprinkled the floor with cloves and dried orange peel, trying to mask the unpleasant stench in the air. Cirrus finally recognized the smell: it reminded him of the times Mrs. Kickshaw left her meat pies in the oven too long. The stink of charred flesh.

Cirrus ran his fingers along the electrostatic machine. "What exactly does it do?" he asked, glancing up at his friend. Just the sight of the glass wheels made his heart race faster.

Bottle Top shrugged. "Sends lightning through my body, I suppose."

Cirrus gasped. "Does it hurt?"

"Not really," said Bottle Top. "Just takes some getting used to is all. Starts off as a slight tingle, then sharpens into a sting. Only the end is painful—like a million hot needles piercing your skin all at once."

Cirrus's eyes widened, but Bottle Top reassured him with a smile. "It's worth it, though, for the coin at the end."

Cirrus looked around him. "What about Micah?" he said.

Bottle Top smirked. "Micah don't always get what he wants."

Mr. Leechcraft now reappeared onstage and clapped his hands. "Boys, boys! It's time to greet our guests. The carriages are arriving."

Immediately the other boys grabbed their candles and filed from the room. Cirrus found a quiet place behind the stage to sit and wait, and watched as Bottle Top swayed back and forth in the gloom.

A short while later people began to take their seats.

Cirrus, concealed in the shadows, stared from face to face. He had never seen such well-dressed people. There were elegant ladies with bows in their hair, shriveled old women with jewels round their throats, and stiff, military-looking gentlemen.

Mr. Leechcraft entered behind them.

"Esteemed and honored guests," he said, stepping onto the stage and greeting the audience with a low bow, "I take great pleasure in welcoming you to my humble establishment, the Hall of Wonders."

One or two of the ladies yawned, someone coughed and fans began to flutter in mute applause. Mr. Leechcraft, however, seemed undaunted.

"Aether," he said, letting the word hang in the air like a puff of smoke. "Invisible, weightless, it binds all things together, holds everything in its place. Like the breath breathed into Adam, it is the key to our existence. . . ."

From his vantage point behind the stage, Cirrus could see Micah, Daniel, Ezekiel and Job strapping themselves into special thronelike chairs around the edges of the auditorium. One by one, they extinguished their candle flames and lowered what looked like large transparent crowns onto their heads. Soon, only a few small moths of light were wriggling onstage, next to Mr. Leechcraft, who had lowered his voice to a near-whisper.

"Ladies and gentlemen," he said, so softly that Cirrus, like the rest of the audience, had to lean forward to hear, "prepare to be astounded, amazed. For tonight, before your very eyes, I shall endeavor to make the unknown known . . . and DARKNESS VISIBLE!"

His voice built to a sudden crescendo and, with a final, dramatic gesture, he quenched the remaining flames onstage, plunging the room into shadow.

And then, very eerily, the edges of the auditorium began to glow. . . .

Someone shrieked and another person hollered. Even Cirrus let out a frightened gasp. For the specially constructed spheres that the boys had lowered onto their heads had, like halos, started to shine. Miniature firestorms crackled and sputtered inside the globes while the boys themselves sat as still as saints.

"Behold," said Mr. Leechcraft, "the wonder of my Beatified Boys!"

Soon the entire audience was twisting round to stare in astonishment at the strangely glowing boys. Applause filled the room.

A vicious *snap* tore across the stage, and each and every head whipped round. Cirrus clapped a hand to his heart, afraid. For, while everyone had been distracted, Mr. Leechcraft had cranked the handle of his machine and summoned a stroke of lightning from the air!

"Aether," said Mr. Leechcraft, once all eyes were fixed again on him. "It is in the air we breathe, the matter we touch. It can be used to nurture and to destroy. . . ."

Now began a series of experiments the likes of which Cirrus had never seen. While he and the audience watched, Mr. Leechcraft made paper figurines dance on metal plates, lit candles with nothing more than vials of water and even ignited a rabbit's bladder, which soared above the stage on a string of flame before erupting into volcanic fire.

And then, just when Cirrus was beginning to tire of all the effects, snowflakes drifted to the ground. He glanced up to see Bottle Top scattering a pail of goose feathers.

"And now see what spirit we can summon from an innocent child," said Mr. Leechcraft, as Bottle Top began his descent on the swing. "Behold! Cupid with the Sparkling Kiss!"

The audience burst into rapturous applause as Bottle Top finally made his entrance. For a moment it seemed to Cirrus as though all the birds in the aviary had been set free, as women cooed and cawed and flapped their fans. And then something else caught his eye: a gentleman seated near the back of the theater, a diminutive figure in a chair on wheels. He was holding a lens and leaning forward to get a better view of the boy onstage.

Cirrus felt a knot of apprehension in his stomach as he realized this was almost certainly the gentleman Mr. Leechcraft was so keen to impress. The gentleman from the Guild.

A sudden flash of lightning turned his attention back to the performance. Mr. Leechcraft had sent another pulse of energy across the room, just inches away from Bottle Top's swing. The women in the audience let out a horrified cry.

"Remember," said Mr. Leechcraft, with a cruel, dark smile. "Aether can be used for good or for ill. It can nurture just as easily as it can destroy."

One of the women now leapt out of her seat, eager to save

Bottle Top from his apparent fate, but Bottle Top merely smiled and reassured her that she need not worry.

"See?" he said, offering her his hand, which was calm and steady. "I am not scared."

She clutched his fingers and offered him a coin. Bottle Top turned his head toward Cirrus with a satisfied grin; Micah, however, in control of the ropes, glared.

Swallowing the lump in his throat, Cirrus now watched as Mr. Leechcraft made a great show of removing the gun barrel from the front of the electrostatic machine and then, very carefully, aligning the soles of Bottle Top's feet with the glass wheels instead.

A hush fell upon the audience.

Mr. Leechcraft stepped back to the handle and the disks began to spin.

A slow, soft hiss filled the air.

Cirrus could not take his eyes off Bottle Top, who was lying perfectly still, his face serene. He remembered what Bottle Top had told him about the needling pain, and his hands started to sweat.

Then, when Cirrus could stand the tension no longer and expected Bottle Top at any moment to explode in a flash of flame, Bottle Top held out his hands and, as if by magic, all of the feathers that had scattered to the stage floated up through the air. They clung to his skin. Bottle Top had become a human magnet!

Cirrus joined in the applause rolling over the stage like

a wave. Bottle Top delighted the audience with a beaming grin.

"Behold, the miracles of Nature in the hands of a child," said Mr. Leechcraft, who continued to crank the handle. "Now see what other spirits we can coax from his soul."

The wheels turned faster and the audience grew restless once again. Cirrus, concerned, could see the strain beginning to show on Bottle Top's face. Beads of perspiration slipped down his brow and his brand-new teeth were clenched in pain. Still Mr. Leechcraft did not relent, but continued to turn the handle, round and round.

At last, little cobwebs of light began to appear between Bottle Top's fingers and, in a sudden flash, a bolt of energy shot across the stage, striking a brass sphere several feet away. The audience shrieked, drowning out Bottle Top's tiny yelp of pain.

Cirrus glanced anxiously at his friend, who was trying not to flinch as tears slid down his cheeks.

"I present you, ladies and gentlemen, with the true spark of life," said Mr. Leechcraft, taking a deep long bow. "The Breath of God, if you will."

The audience burst again into applause.

As soon as the ovation had ended, Mr. Leechcraft invited a lady onstage. "Madam, would you care to kiss an angel?" he said gallantly, extending a hand.

He escorted a short, plump woman to a footstool before Bottle Top's swing. Bottle Top squirmed when he saw her.

She was old and haggard, with a beauty spot the size of a squashed insect on her chin. She withdrew a coin from her purse and placed it in his palm, then closed her eyes and puckered her lips. She leaned forward to give Bottle Top a kiss.

Mr. Leechcraft immediately leapt back to the machine and cranked the handle. Moments later a sharp bee sting of light snapped from Bottle Top's lips and the woman exclaimed in pain. She swooned to the floor, while Bottle Top dabbed a finger to his still-healing gums.

The audience roared with laughter and rose, as one, to its feet.

The performance over, the guests now began to take their leave. Ezekiel and Job held their candles aloft to guide them through the darkened museum.

Mr. Leechcraft, meanwhile, rushed directly to the man from the Guild. "Pray, sir, what did you think of our performance?" he said.

Mr. Sidereal said nothing, but continued staring at the stage, where Bottle Top was waiting to be let down from the swing. Instead of releasing him, however, Micah skittered across the stage and turned the handle of the machine, sending yet more energy through the soles of the boy's feet.

Cirrus launched himself from the shadows to release his friend.

No sooner had he stepped on the footstool, however, than a flash of lightning struck him full in the chest. He was knocked hard to the ground and cracked his head on the boards.

For a moment he lay perfectly still, aware of a splintering pain, and then he noticed a shimmering light swirling above him, floating up from his chest.

Terrified, he scrabbled at his clothes, thinking he was on fire, and found to his astonishment that the sphere under his jacket had come undone. It was releasing an icy blue-and-white vapor into the air. With fumbling fingers, he managed to thread the halves together and breathed a sigh of relief as, slowly, gradually, the light around him began to fade.

He staggered to his feet.

Everyone was staring at the waning drifts of light—all except Bottle Top, who was slumped on the floor. He had been blown clear off his swing.

"Are you hurt?" cried Cirrus, rushing over to him, but Bottle Top cowered and backed away. He was rubbing his left elbow and whimpering in pain. His wings had been crushed beneath him in the fall.

"I'm sorry," said Cirrus, shaking all over. "I don't know what happened."

Helplessly, he turned to Mr. Leechcraft, who seemed equally perplexed. Only Mr. Sidereal showed no surprise. He was staring intently at Cirrus's chest.

"That boy," he said, in a high, nasal voice. "Bring him to me."

Mr. Leechcraft pointed at Cirrus, who nervously approached.

Mr. Sidereal looked him straight in the eye.

"What is your name?" he asked, and reached out to stroke Cirrus's jacket.

Cirrus automatically drew back.

"Why, he is my new Hanging Boy," said Mr. Leechcraft quickly, before Cirrus had a chance to speak. He hooked his fingers round the boy's shoulders and clutched him tightly to his breast. "I have been training him with my other boys. Only, I was not certain the time had yet come to display him."

"Well, the time is at hand," said Mr. Sidereal. "He must be exhibited before the Guild at once."

Mr. Leechcraft blinked.

"The Guild, sir?"

"But of course! This boy is full of Aether! Can you not see it? The Guild will be most interested in this remarkable child."

Cirrus glanced uneasily at Bottle Top, who was staring at him savagely from the stage.

Mr. Leechcraft appeared stunned. "When, erm, do you intend to exhibit him, sir?"

"Tomorrow night," said Mr. Sidereal, clawing at the armrests of his chair. "The Guild will be meeting then."

Cirrus felt as if he was going to faint. He hoped for a moment that the man might decline the invitation, but Mr. Leechcraft seemed to pull himself together.

"Tomorrow night will be fine, sir," he said, much to Cirrus's horror.

"Good. I shall see to it that everything is arranged," said Mr. Sidereal. He began to wheel his chair away.

At once, Mr. Leechcraft called Micah and Bottle Top forward to help the gentleman. Cirrus cast another frightened look at his friend, but Bottle Top stormed right past him and did not look back.

❧ 19 ❧

The Fallen Angel

Pandora stood in the garden outside the Hall of Wonders and stared up at the museum. Torches flared on either side of the main entrance, but the windows were as dark as pewter and showed no signs of life.

"Where is he? What is keeping him so long?" she asked, pacing up and down the gravel paths.

"Patience, Pandora," said a voice from behind her.

She turned. Mr. Hardy was perched on the edge of a large stone plinth in the center of the square, almost as still as the statue above him. His spyglass was raised to his eye and his sights were fixed on the doorway.

All day long they had been watching Mr. Sidereal. While ash-colored clouds gathered over the city and thunder rolled across the sky, they had stood on a sweltering street corner outside his observatory, waiting for him to lead them to the boy.

Finally, as the sun began to set, igniting the sky with a coppery haze, Mr. Sidereal had left his residence in a gilded carriage. Mr. Hardy had immediately given chase in a shabby black coach he had hired for the purpose. The coachman took the corners at a trot, allowing them to keep up with the fancy carriage.

A short while later they had pulled up outside a building on the north side of Leicester Fields. Pandora had exclaimed in delight when she saw the statue of the horse and rider in the middle of the square.

"Mr. Hardy!" she cried, clasping him by the arm. "This is where I saw him last. I'm almost certain of it. Mr. Sidereal must know where Cirrus is!"

But rather than following Mr. Sidereal inside, as she had wanted to do, they had taken up a position outside the museum to wait. It was safer to remain hidden, Mr. Hardy said, than to barge right in. Besides, he had taken one look at the printed notice outside the door and fallen into a strangely dark humor. A deep line worried his brow.

Sighing with frustration, Pandora stepped away from the statue and advanced once more toward the garden gate.

"Careful, Pandora," said Mr. Hardy.

His lens was still fixed on the door.

"I shan't go far," she promised, and crept along the path.

Numerous carriages had drawn up to the museum's entrance and she could hear the horses snorting and shifting in the dark.

She moved closer.

Then, just as she reached the edge of the lawn, the door to the Hall of Wonders opened and light poured forth. She pressed herself to the railing and kept very still as two thin boys in matching uniforms led an entourage of men and women down the steps.

Voices carried through the air.

"Such a cherubic boy. I do hope he was not much hurt. . . ."

"Nonsense, my dear. It was all a trick of the light."

She watched as the party picked its way over the paving stones and, one by one, the carriages drove off. The two boys raced back to the museum, where they promptly disappeared.

There was still no sign of Mr. Sidereal or the boy Cirrus Flux.

Pandora sighed, wondering if her suspicions had been wrong. Perhaps Mr. Sidereal did not know where the boy was after all.

Her mind flashed back to Alerion, whom they had left on the rooftop of St. Paul's. She longed to be by the fiery bird's side, basking in the warm glow of her feathers.

Finally, after an agony of waiting, Pandora saw the door open once again. This time, Mr. Sidereal appeared. Several boys were stooped under the weight of his chair, which they carried down the steps. A little boy in a powdered wig and what looked like damaged angel wings followed a short distance behind.

Pandora glanced at Mr. Hardy, who was virtually invisible in the night. He signaled for her to remain out of sight.

Pandora planted herself in the shadows and turned her attention back to the door.

Two figures were now framed by the light in the hall: a lean, wolfish gentleman in a dark gray wig and a curly-haired boy. Cirrus Flux!

Her heart skipped a beat when she saw him, and it took a great force of will for her not to shout out. She wanted to leap forward and grab him by the arm, but the man was holding him very tightly, she noticed, and Cirrus looked frightened and pale. He was clutching the buttons of his jacket. Not once did his eyes leave the man in the chair.

"Until tomorrow night," she heard Mr. Sidereal say, as the boys carried him over the ground. "I shall send my carriage to collect you and take you to the Guild."

"Why, yes, sir. Thank you, sir," said the man at the door.

Pandora's brow furrowed. What were they planning? Where was this Guild?

"Yes, yes. Just remember to bring the boy," said Mr. Sidereal.

"Do not worry, sir. I shall not let him out of my sight."

She glanced once more at Mr. Hardy, wondering if he would spring into action and save the boy, but his face was dark and inscrutable, and his spyglass did not stray from the door. By the time she turned round, the man and the boy had gone back into the museum.

Mr. Sidereal was just on the other side of the railing now, less than a stone's throw away, and she could hear the boys' labored breathing as they carried him across the paving stones. She crouched even lower and watched as the driver got down from his seat and opened the door for the gentleman, who was lifted inside. An oil lamp, fitted into the compartment, jeweled the interior with light.

The four boys, relieved of their duty, stepped back and, with a brief bow to Mr. Sidereal, scuttled away. Only the boy with the crumpled angel wings remained. He lingered a moment, inspecting the carriage, and then he, too, turned away.

Mr. Sidereal called him back.

The boy hesitated.

"Yes, you," said Mr. Sidereal in a high-pitched voice. "I'd like a word in your ear."

The boy moved closer.

Pandora, crouched next to the iron railing, watched as the boy glanced nervously from side to side and then approached the golden carriage. At the man's behest, he climbed inside and closed the door. Cocooned in silence, they started to talk.

Pandora leaned closer, straining to overhear what was said, but the driver was standing next to the carriage and she could not creep any nearer without being caught. Through the window of the carriage, however, she could see the man motioning to his neck. The little boy nodded and pointed to his chest.

A nasty smile crept over Mr. Sidereal's lips.

They continued to talk.

Judging from the way the boy kept glancing at the museum, Pandora guessed their discussion must have something to do with Cirrus Flux.

Finally, Mr. Sidereal reached into his coat and pulled out a small leather purse. He withdrew several gold coins that glittered in his hand.

The boy's eyes widened and his fingers wrestled in his lap. He stared at the money and then at the man. Eventually, he nodded.

Another smile crept over Mr. Sidereal's lips.

Pandora ducked into hiding as the carriage door opened and the boy got out.

"Tomorrow night, at the Guild," she heard Mr. Sidereal say. "You know where to find me."

The boy turned and nodded, then cautiously extended his hand.

Mr. Sidereal frowned.

"Of course," he said, pressing a few coins into the boy's palm. He grabbed the boy's wrist and pulled him even closer. "Do not try to deceive me," he hissed. "You will receive the remainder when I have what I seek."

He let go of the boy's hand and the driver immediately shut the door and leapt up onto his seat. The carriage bounded forward.

The boy paused for a moment, fingering his wrist, and then headed slowly back to the museum.

Pandora hurried over to Mr. Hardy. "I do not trust them,"

she said, brooding over everything she had seen. "I think they're planning something. The boy in the carriage—I think Mr. Sidereal was asking him about the sphere."

Mr. Hardy nodded, but did not reply. He was taking long marching strides across the square.

"I heard them mention the Guild," she added. "Something about tomorrow night."

Still Mr. Hardy said nothing.

Pandora struggled to keep up. "Mr. Hardy," she said at last, "is there something wrong?"

Finally, he stopped. "Aye," he said. "The owner of the museum. I've seen him before."

"Who is he?"

Mr. Hardy glared. "Goes by the name of Leechcraft. He's one of those who shot the birds for sport."

Pandora thought again of Alerion waiting for them and went cold all over. A shiver rippled down her spine. "What are we going to do, Mr. Hardy?" she asked, worry creeping into her voice.

"We're going to take to the skies," he said, "and watch the Guild like a hawk."

❧ 20 ❧

The Celestial Chamber

Cirrus stepped away from the small garret window at the top of the Hall of Wonders and checked his reflection in the mirror on the wall. Gone were his coarse brown foundling's clothes and in their place he now wore an emerald-green jacket, fancy breeches and silver-buckled shoes. His hair had been carefully powdered and tied back with a bow. Mrs. Kickshaw, he thought gloomily, missing her all of a sudden, would be proud.

Behind him, the other boys were wrestling on the beds they shared in the corner. Only Bottle Top took no part. He was sitting on his own, picking feathers from the wings that lay discarded on his lap.

Cirrus walked over to him. "I'm sorry," he said, for the hundredth time. "I didn't mean for this to happen, I promise. I wish I didn't have to take part."

Bottle Top glanced up at him with bruised-looking eyes,

but said nothing. Instead, he rose from his seat and crossed to the other side of the room. He was still nursing his arm, which was bound in a sling.

Cirrus sat on the edge of the bed. He was not certain what had caused the sphere round his neck to react as it had the night before, but he was glad that it had stopped glowing. He had not dared open it again, just in case the other boys were around to watch. He had even slept with it under his pillow, tucked in the palm of his hand. He wondered how he would be able to keep it a secret from the Guild.

His mind was full of unanswered questions. Where had his father found it? What was it for? One thing, however, was certain. Whatever it contained was powerful; it had blown Bottle Top clear off his swing, after all.

A bell rang from below and Cirrus followed the other boys down the steep wooden steps to the hall. He took them slowly, one at a time, feeling the knot in his stomach tighten the closer he got to the door.

"Boys, boys!" said Mr. Leechcraft, as they gathered round. "Tonight we are to perform at the Guild of Empirical Science. This is a tremendous honor for us, a rare privilege indeed, and it is of vital importance you do as you're told."

He outlined the performance—how Cirrus was to replace Bottle Top as the new Hanging Boy—and then escorted them out through the door, where a gilded carriage, driven by six white horses, had arrived.

"Ah, Mr. Sidereal has sent his finest carriage, I see," said Mr. Leechcraft, with a satisfied smile.

Dark clouds had gathered overhead, trapping the light in a resinous haze. Dust hovered in the air.

Cirrus looked around him uneasily. "Where is Mr. Sidereal?" he asked, unable to forget the meaningful look the man had given him the night before. Once again he tapped the sphere under his shirt to make sure that it was safely hidden.

"Mr. Sidereal sends his apologies," said Mr. Leechcraft. "He will meet us there."

Cirrus climbed into the carriage, followed by the other boys. Mr. Leechcraft squeezed in beside them, a rich, musky odor emanating from his clothes. He had doused himself in ambergris in honor of the occasion tonight.

"Why, even the streets are paved with gold," he remarked happily, observing the amber glow in the air.

The carriage started forward with a jolt.

Cirrus wanted to draw the curtains, to close himself off in the dark, but Mr. Leechcraft insisted on driving with the windows open, providing them with a view of the crowds. Mr. Leechcraft gave a regal salute as they passed. A smile seemed stitched to his lips.

Cirrus glanced at Bottle Top, who was sitting opposite, chewing on an angry muscle in his cheek. Gladly would he have swapped places with him, if only he could, but Mr. Leechcraft had clasped him by the elbow and wouldn't let go. All day long he had been referring to him as "my new Golden Boy." Cirrus squirmed in his seat.

A short while later they pulled up to a large building on the shore of the Thames. Already a multitude of people had assembled on the steps: officers in dark blue uniforms and merchants in jewel-colored silks. Carriages plugged the lanes.

"Even the Astronomer Royal is here," said Mr. Leechcraft in an excited whisper, looking around.

There was still no sign, however, of Mr. Sidereal himself.

Cirrus felt the queasy feeling in his stomach slide into his bowels as they crossed the square. Above them the sky was steadily darkening and he could feel the threat of thunder in the air. A storm was brewing.

He was grateful when, at last, they entered the cool quiet of the hall. A parade of marble busts lined the walls: old, venerable gentlemen, reminding him of the Governor at the hospital. Just for a moment he longed to feel Mr. Chalfont by his side, but Mr. Leechcraft was there instead. He hooked Cirrus by the elbow and steered him toward the stairs.

"Micah, Daniel, Ezekiel, Job," said the gentleman, once the other boys had settled down; they had found a large globe in the corner, which they were spinning. "You will remain here and greet the guests. They are all educated men, well versed in the mysteries of science, so there is to be no foolishness, do you understand? Everything depends upon your good behavior tonight. Meanwhile, our Golden Boy here"—he patted Cirrus on the shoulder, making him blush—"shall perform in the Celestial Chamber upstairs."

"Sir," said Bottle Top suddenly, "may I help him prepare?"

Mr. Leechcraft regarded him with a look of surprise, as though he had forgotten his existence until now.

"Yes, yes. That will be fine, Abraham," he said. "Go ahead."

For a moment Cirrus wondered if their friendship had been restored, but then Bottle Top brushed past him and rushed up the stairs.

Cirrus followed more slowly, taking his time.

Tier upon tier of wooden balustrades overlooked the hall, which was decorated with oil paintings and lit by glittering chandeliers. Each floor appeared to be dedicated to a different branch of empirical science. Tall, ticking clocks and sophisticated pieces of equipment stood against the walls. The air had an ancient, dusty smell.

Finally they came to a pair of imposing doors with a godlike hand carved into the wood. The Celestial Chamber, Cirrus guessed. Bottle Top nudged a door open with his shoulder and went in.

Cirrus found himself looking into a vast chamber with a raised glass ceiling that provided a spectacular view of the sky. Clouds rolled overhead, pulling and tearing apart like waves. Cirrus thought he glimpsed a ball of lightning, but it promptly disappeared.

"You will descend from there," said Mr. Leechcraft, entering behind them and indicating a swing that had been erected under the middle of the glass. "And I shall electrify you here."

He pointed to a gleaming gun barrel that had been positioned next to a broad oak table and a row of chairs. It was

253

nearly twice as long as the one in the Hall of Wonders and attached to a bright metal sphere. Unlike the machine in the museum, however, it was connected to a number of tall, dark gray jars.

Mr. Leechcraft caught him looking.

"Mr. Sidereal has kindly provided us with his supply of Leyden jars," he explained, "which, he assures me, contain a charge far superior to my own. Just imagine: soon lightning itself will be coursing through your veins! It will produce a most scintillating effect!"

Cirrus felt his mind go numb. All he could think of was what Bottle Top had told him before: being electrified felt like a million hot needles piercing your skin all at once.

"Will it hurt?" he asked, his voice sounding timid and small.

"Nonsense, my boy. A little discomfort never troubled a child," said Mr. Leechcraft.

Cirrus glanced at Bottle Top, who was staring at the floor.

"There, you see?" said Mr. Leechcraft. "It will be a mild stabbing sensation, nothing more."

At this moment Ezekiel burst into the room. "Mr. Leechcraft, you must come quick, sir," he said. He was clutching his chest and panting. "There's gentlemen arriving. They're coming up the stairs."

"Heavens!" said Mr. Leechcraft, consulting a pocket watch. "We must delay them at once." He turned to Bottle Top. "Whatever are you waiting for? Help the boy into his harness and hoist him into the air."

Without another word, he left.

Bottle Top moved toward the rope and started lowering the swing to the floor. "Take off your shoes and lie down," he said to Cirrus finally, without looking up.

Cirrus did as he was told. Following Bottle Top's example from the night before, he slid onto the swing, which rocked back and forth. The board pressed into his stomach, which was bubbling with nerves.

"I wish I didn't have to do this," he said again as Bottle Top adjusted the straps round his waist.

Bottle Top, however, said nothing and pulled the cords tight.

"Careful! They're pinching me," said Cirrus, reaching out behind him to loosen the straps.

Suddenly, Bottle Top grabbed hold of both his wrists and wrenched them behind his back. He forced them under the straps of the harness and bound them to the swing.

Cirrus grunted with surprise. "What are you doing?" he cried, desperately trying to wriggle free. "Are you mad?"

But Bottle Top ignored him and yanked on the straps.

Jagged pain tore across Cirrus's shoulder blades, making him wince.

"Bottle Top, please!" said Cirrus, fear edging into his voice. "What are you doing? I didn't mean for this to happen, if that's what you think!"

He angled his head toward the doorway and shouted, "Help! Help!" But Mr. Leechcraft was too far away to hear now and a loud clap of thunder drowned out the sound of his voice.

Finally, Bottle Top stepped out to where Cirrus could see him clearly. He had removed the sling from his arm and was twisting the bolt of cloth into a knot. He was not as injured as he had made out.

Cirrus's eyes bulged with fright. He watched helplessly as Bottle Top inserted the sling into his mouth and secured the ends with a tight knot. The moist cloth blocked the back of his throat and he had to inhale wildly through his nose.

"Bottle Top, please!" he tried to shout, but his voice came out as a muffled sob.

Bottle Top averted his eyes. "I'm sorry, Cirrus," he said at last, loosening the collar of Cirrus's shirt and carefully removing the sphere from the boy's neck. "But Mr. Sidereal offered me far more than I could refuse for this." He held up the sphere and looked at it with only mild interest before placing it under his own shirt for safekeeping. "He's going to make me rich."

Bottle Top stepped behind him now and began pulling on the ropes. Cirrus felt the swing judder and rise. Within moments, he was dangling a few feet below the ceiling, underneath the glass, while lightning whipped and flashed across the sky.

"Goodbye, Cirrus," said Bottle Top, still refusing to meet his eye. He slowly made his way across the room and left. He did not look back.

Cirrus wriggled and twisted, but the bonds were too tight. Hot spasms of pain fired down his back. There was no escape. Even if he managed to break free from the harness, the fall would almost certainly shatter his legs. All he could do was wait for Mr. Leechcraft to return and then beg to be let down.

A terrifying thought suddenly occurred to him. What if Mr. Leechcraft ignored his request and tried to electrify him instead? What if he generated a bolt of lightning, the way he had with Bottle Top the previous night?

Cirrus eyed the Leyden jars uneasily and resumed his struggle to escape.

Just then a tremendous clap of thunder exploded overhead. Startled, he twisted his neck and peered up through the glass. Clouds were churning above him, scratched by silver claws of light.

Then, out of the corner of his eye, he saw something streaking toward him, blazing across the sky. It looked like a giant ball of flame.

He blinked as the object grew bigger and brighter, blotting out the entire sky. It was heading straight for him . . . and would any moment smash through the glass.

Cirrus braced for the impact, closing his eyes.

❧ 21 ❧

Escape!

"**M**r. Hardy!" shouted Pandora over a near-deafening clap of thunder, as a flash of lightning lit up the sky. "It's the boy from last night! He's headed across the square!"

All evening long she and Mr. Hardy had been circling the city in the moon-sail, keeping a close watch on the Guild, but there had been no sign of Mr. Sidereal, who had sent his golden carriage to pick up the boys from the museum, but who himself had not arrived.

Mr. Hardy shifted his weight in the basket and steered the moon-sail into a trough of cold air, bringing them down low over the Guild. The wind slammed into their bodies and shrilled in their ears, and Pandora had to cling to the ropes to keep from falling down.

They were just in time to see the boy hop into Mr. Sidereal's carriage before the vehicle pulled away, galloping east along the Strand toward St. Paul's.

Mr. Hardy made as if to follow, but Pandora grabbed him by the arm. "What about Cirrus?" she cried. "We can't just leave him behind! He could be in trouble!"

Mr. Hardy yelled something that was lost in reply, and Pandora feared he was not going to listen, but then Alerion burst into flame and the moon-sail soared again into the sky, riding a powerful air current back over the Guild.

Pandora fixed Mr. Hardy's spyglass to her eye, searching the many windows for a glimpse of the boy. All she could see were glimmering candles and reflections of the lightning-torn sky.

Then, as they passed high overhead, she noticed a window set in the roof of the Guild. She could just make out a small figure beneath it, dangling in the air.

"Mr. Hardy!" she called out, and pointed below. "Look there! It's Cirrus!"

Mr. Hardy leaned over the edge of the basket and peered down. "Hold on," he said as Alerion folded her wings and the moon-sail plummeted once again.

This time the wind snatched the cap from Pandora's head and her short auburn curls flew out behind.

The basket landed with a hard, heavy thump on the side of the window, sending a large web of cracks through the glass. Almost immediately, the wind shifted direction and swept them back into the air.

"Mr. Hardy!" screamed Pandora, as they began to ascend.

But the man was ready. Grabbing the anchor from the side of the basket, he dropped it through the glass, into the furthest corner of the room, and the window shattered into a million fragments that rained to the floor, narrowly missing the boy.

Cirrus looked up at them with terrified eyes and tried even harder to break free from his bonds. The anchor was swinging recklessly back and forth, banging into a table, knocking over some chairs.

Mr. Hardy turned to Pandora. "Quick! Climb down the rope and secure the anchor. Untie the boy and I'll haul you up!"

Pandora stared at him incredulously and then peered over the ledge. It was a thirty-foot drop, at least. Her stomach revolted inside her.

"I can't," she cried. "It's too far. You go instead."

Mr. Hardy glanced at the moon-sail and shook his head. "The wind is too strong. We haven't much time!"

A mass of dark cloud had piled overhead and violent downdrafts of air tugged at them from the Thames. The sky had taken on a terrible greenish gray pallor.

Pandora was shaking from head to foot, but Mr. Hardy grasped her by the shoulders and steadied her with his eyes.

"You can do this, Pandora," he told her firmly. "I've seen you climb the wall of the Foundling Hospital, don't forget."

She braved a false smile and took a deep breath. Finally, she nodded.

"Aye, that's my girl," said Mr. Hardy.

With his help, she reached over the edge of the basket

and took a tentative hold of the rope, which was lashing beneath her. Slowly, carefully, she began her descent.

The wind twirled around her, screaming in her ears, but she clung onto the rope with work-hardened fingers and eased her way down.

"That's it, Pandora!" yelled Mr. Hardy, guiding her from above. "You're almost there."

She breathed a sigh of relief as she passed through the shattered window, into the relative calm of the room. Cirrus was a short distance from her, squirming in midair. His arms had been bound behind him and his mouth had been gagged. His face was slick with sweat.

"Don't worry," she said, quickening her pace. "I'll let you down."

As soon as she was able, she dropped to the ground. At once she grabbed the arm of the anchor and secured it to the table, fixing the moon-sail in place. Then she dashed to the pulley in the corner and started lowering the boy to the floor. She removed the gag from his mouth.

"It's you!" he said, gasping for air. "How did you . . . ? What're you . . . ?"

Pandora was loosening the straps that bound him to the swing. Then, all of a sudden, she covered his mouth with her hand. "Shhh!" she said.

She listened carefully. Voices were rising from downstairs. Immediately, she started unpicking the rest of the straps.

Her fingers were trembling and the bonds were too tight.

In desperation, she looked around for a sharp piece of glass to use as a knife.

"Hold still," she said, as she sawed through the fastenings.

Finally, the last bond snapped loose and Cirrus slumped to the ground. Tenderly, he rubbed the spots where the harness had cut into his skin and kneaded the stiffness from his limbs. He limped toward the door.

Pandora pulled him back. "No, not that way," she cried, and pointed up.

The boy turned to her in alarm and then peered up at the sky, where the moon-sail was visible, buffeting back and forth. Mr. Hardy was leaning over the edge, urging them to hurry.

Seeing him, Cirrus shrank back in terror. "I can't," he said. "That man—you don't understand—I've seen him before. He's after my sphere." He clutched the spot where his token had been and looked ill.

Pandora grabbed hold of his wrist. The straps had left a raw, savage mark on his skin and he winced.

"Listen," she said. "Mr. Hardy's a friend. He knew your father. He's here to help. Now hook your legs over the anchor and he'll hoist you up!"

She yanked the anchor out from under the table and forced it into his hands.

"A friend?" he said, confusion growing on his face.

The babble of voices was getting louder on the stairs.

"Please!" said Pandora. "There's no time to explain. You've got to trust me."

Cirrus started to protest, but then, remembering how the girl had tried to help him at the hospital, he did as she said. Planting his legs on either side of the anchor, he hugged the metal crossbar to his chest. Almost immediately, the man began to haul him up—pulling him, hand over hand, toward the roof.

Pandora, meanwhile, searched for something heavy to barricade the door. She grabbed a tall, straight-backed chair from beside the table and dragged it across the floor, angling it under the handles of the twin wooden doors.

Cirrus was now through the open window and swinging in the air. Dark clouds were thrashing overhead; the storm was growing more intense.

Heart in mouth, she watched as Mr. Hardy reached over the edge of the basket to drag him in.

At that instant, the moon-sail, freed from its mooring, drifted away. It lifted from the roof and headed toward the clouds. Pandora let out a moan of dismay as the boy and the man disappeared.

She spun round to face the door, on her own.

Footsteps had now reached the landing and she drew in a sharp breath as the ornate handles began to turn. The door inched open—

—and then stopped.

The chair had dug in its heels and become stuck.

There was an exclamation of surprise and then an oath from the other side. Someone hammered on the door.

"What is the meaning of this? Boy, open up!"

Pandora backed away from the door. Her heart was beating against her ribs. She kept her eyes fixed on the ceiling, waiting for the moon-sail to reappear.

Lightning streaked across the sky and thunder clapped, but there was no sign of the vessel. Mr. Hardy was not coming back.

Someone slammed a shoulder against the door, making her jump. The chair skipped a few inches and a purple sleeve wedged itself through the gap.

It was the dark-wigged gentleman from the museum. She could just make out his loathsome features through the crack.

"Wait till I get my hands on you," he snarled, clawing at the chair with his hand.

The chair began to give way with a screech.

She took one last look at the sky. Just then a luminous sail of fabric drifted overhead.

"Pandora!" shouted Mr. Hardy, dropping the anchor through the remains of the shattered window. It clanged to the floor. "Grab hold!"

Pandora nearly cried with relief. She lunged for the rope and caught it mid-stride, jamming her foot down hard on the metal crossbar and starting to climb, not even waiting for Mr. Hardy to haul her up.

Behind her she heard a savage cry. She turned to see the dark-wigged gentleman storm into the chamber. He stopped in confusion and then propelled himself toward her.

"What have you done with my Golden Boy?" he roared.

Pandora was rising quickly now, scrabbling up the rope, but at the very last moment the man leapt onto the table and jumped . . . snagging his fingers around the arms of the trailing anchor. He tried with all his might to drag it down.

"Alerion!" shouted Mr. Hardy as the rope slipped through his fingers and Pandora began to sink once more toward the floor. "Up, girl, up!"

The great bird flapped its wings and sent another wave of heat into the sail, lifting the vessel into the air.

Cirrus, who had only just managed to stumble to his feet, fell down again as the basket climbed steeply upward. Pandora was pulled through the open window.

She looked down.

The man below her had refused to let go; with a fearful cry, he, too, floated into the mouth of the storm.

Below them, in the Celestial Chamber, the members of the Guild crowded round the shattered window and gaped, unable to take their eyes off the moon-sail, which was rising rapidly toward the clouds. Only one person bolted from the room: a woman with elaborately coiled silver hair. Madame Orrery! Pandora gasped when she saw her and nearly let go of the rope.

The moon-sail was ascending quickly, lifted by a swell of warm air, but the basket was teetering at a crazy angle, tilting toward the ground. Pandora could see the slate-gray roof tiles of the Guild sloping beneath her and tightened her grip on the rope, which was creaking ominously under the additional weight.

"Let go, you fool!" shouted Mr. Hardy at the man, who was kicking and flailing below them. "You'll kill us all! We can't carry this much cargo!"

But the man refused to let go. He had hooked his arms round the base of the anchor. "Help me! Oh, dear God, help me!" he cried, as the wind ripped off his wig and tore at his clothes. The folds of his long purple coat flew out behind.

The moon-sail was lurching over the river and Pandora caught a whiff of the foul, smelly water: a filthy soup of sewage and bits of timber. Sweat greased her palms and she squeezed her eyes shut, unable to look.

The extra weight on the moon-sail, however, was beginning to take its toll. Alerion, tiring, was unable to keep them away from the downdrafts of air and Pandora could sense the vessel sinking in a slow, steady spiral toward the waves.

She had no choice: She had to climb higher.

Taking a deep breath, she pulled herself up, grimacing with the effort. All of her muscles were straining, her tired fingers ached, but she fed the rope between her tightly locked ankles and inched her way up.

Cirrus was leaning over the edge of the basket, urging her on, reaching out a hand to assist her, even though she was still too far away. Mr. Hardy, meanwhile, was throwing sandbags over the opposite side of the basket, trying desperately to even out their weight. Alerion was furiously flapping her wings.

Pandora could sense the waves slapping beneath her.

A sudden change in the tension of the rope caused her to look down.

The man from the museum had propped his feet on the bar of the anchor and was clawing up the rope.

His face sharpened into a sneer of contempt. "Thieves!" he shouted, gaining courage with every hold. "Give me back my Golden Boy!"

Panic surged through her body and, ignoring the pain in her arms, Pandora forced her way up. The boy was only a few more yards away . . . almost within reach!

But just as her fingers brushed his own, she felt a hand clutch her sharply by the ankle and drag her down. The rope slithered through her fingers, igniting a fire of pain in her palms, and she fell through the air, landing on the gentleman's shoulders.

"Thief!" he snarled again, trying to throw her off. But she kicked out in terror and connected hard with his jaw, leaving him stunned. The man dropped several feet before managing to cling to the rope.

Quickly, before he could recover, she scurried toward Cirrus's waiting hand.

"Mister!" cried Cirrus as he tried, but failed, to pull Pandora in. "I need your help!"

Mr. Hardy immediately turned from the mast, where he was steering the sail through the storm, and, together, they managed to haul Pandora in, almost tipping over the basket. Exhausted, she collapsed into the mound of blankets.

The boy was instantly by her side, feeding her drops of brandy from Mr. Hardy's flask. He appeared to have recovered from some of his shock, although his face was still anxious and pale. He kept casting uneasy glances at the man and the bird, cowering a little whenever Alerion burst into flame.

"Are you all right?" he asked her, propping her head up.

The fiery liquid helped revive her and she nodded, forcing herself once more to her feet.

The moon-sail was no longer tipping at such a crazy angle, but the ropes were protesting under the weight. They were sinking still toward the waves.

"Let go, damn you!" yelled Mr. Hardy at the man from the museum, who was scrambling up the rope.

"Not without my Golden Boy!"

"Very well, you leave me no choice!" Mr. Hardy reached into his pocket and pulled out a sharp knife.

Pandora reached over to stay his hand.

"You can't!" she cried.

"But he's pulling us down. The scoundrel's dead weight!"

"He'll drown!"

"Don't you worry about him," he said to Pandora. "Rats like him can swim." And with that, he severed the rope.

Pandora plugged her ears as the thin, repulsive man hurtled back through the air and crashed into the waves more than a hundred feet below. He disappeared beneath the water, with next to no splash.

"But we need the anchor to land," said Pandora miserably, as the moon-sail soared into the clouds.

The boy was peering down at the dark churning water. "I think he's survived," he said, as a small, slimy figure crawled onto the muddy riverbank.

But before he could say anything else, a clap of thunder exploded overhead and the moon-sail dipped wildly through the sky. Cirrus, leaning over the edge, lost his balance and fell.

❧ 22 ❧

The Breath of God

For a terrifying moment the wind skimmed past his face and buffeted his body as he plunged headlong toward the waves. Then something hot and fiery hooked him by the shoulders and carried him back through the air. He twisted his neck to see the fierce eagle-like creature flapping its wings above him, the heat of its feathers searing into his flesh. It had clasped him firmly in its talons.

The world turned somersaults, and moments later the bird dropped him again in the basket and returned to its perch. Cirrus found himself staring into the face of the man from Black Mary's Hole. Fear flashed through him, but he recalled what the girl had said: the man was a friend.

"Careful," said the man, as the bird lifted them higher into the air. "You may have your father's curls, but you ain't got his sea legs just yet."

There was a hint of humor in his voice, although his eyes were shaded by the brim of his three-cornered hat.

Cirrus struggled to sit upright, but before he could speak, the man said, "Now then, boy. Hand over the sphere."

Cirrus was aware of the girl watching him. She was no longer dressed in her foundling's uniform, but in a short blue jacket and beige trousers instead. He remembered her name: Pandora.

"The sphere," said the man again, breaking into his thoughts. "Have you got it with you?"

"Bottle Top," he muttered feebly, feeling a stab of betrayal. "Bottle Top took it. . . . I thought he was my friend."

The man regarded him blankly for a moment, then realization dawned on his face. "Why, the little devil!" he said to the girl. "It's the boy in the gilded carriage. He's taking the sphere to Mr. Sidereal!"

Immediately, Pandora rushed to the far side of the basket and raised a spyglass to her eye. Cirrus joined her, stepping more clumsily over the blankets that were heaped inside. Once again, he noticed the glossy sail bulging above them, and the cords and cables holding everything in place, and wondered how they were able to stay in the air.

They were above the river still, following a path the wind carved through the sky. London stretched in all directions: a sprawl of darkened buildings and twisting lanes. Most of the streets were deserted, lit by flickering lanterns.

Suddenly, the girl raised her arm and pointed. "Mr. Hardy! I can see the carriage! It's almost there!"

Cirrus followed the direction of her finger—past the wharves and warehouses along the river to the dome of St. Paul's. He could just make out the tail end of a golden carriage streaking past the churchyard, the same carriage he and the other boys had traveled in before.

"Hold on," said Mr. Hardy, grabbing onto the ropes and leaning over the side of the basket, steering them into a channel of cold air.

They dived toward the city.

Cirrus grasped the sides of the basket and accidentally brushed the girl's hand. Here, beneath the clouds, her face was jubilant, alive. Her amber eyes sparkled and her auburn hair flamed.

Embarrassed, he turned away and looked at the bird, which was burning above them, flapping its wings.

"Wonderful, isn't she?" said the girl. "She's a Halcyon Bird, from the other side of the world."

Cirrus suddenly remembered the ashes he had seen at the bottom of the cage in the Hall of Wonders. "Like the one in Mr. Leechcraft's collection?" he said.

The man heard this and scowled. He spat over the edge.

"Mr. Leechcraft was a no-good thief," he said. "A scoundrel. Got what he deserved."

Cirrus cast him a nervous look, but had no time to ask questions, for just as they passed over a ditch, spewing its filth into the Thames, Pandora spotted a dove-gray carriage pursuing them through the lanes.

"Mr. Hardy!" she called out, aiming her spyglass at the ground. "There's a carriage following us. I think it's Madame Orrery. There's a silver timepiece on the door."

Mr. Hardy swore and urged Alerion to a higher elevation, carrying them over the inns and yards below. Cirrus could see the dome of St. Paul's Cathedral rising above the city. Mr. Hardy was steering them straight toward it.

Cirrus stared at him in amazement, marveling at his ability to sail through the air, but then a ferocious clap of thunder cracked overhead and a claw of lightning split the sky, scratching the underbelly of cloud. With a hiss, hail began to fall, whitening the air like sudden winter.

The man glanced up at the sail, concern written all over his face.

"What's wrong?" yelled Cirrus.

"The hail," said the man. "It'll puncture the sail. We'll go down."

"You'd best hold on," said Pandora, grabbing Cirrus's arm. She, too, had gone pale. "Landings can be difficult."

Cirrus looked around at the tightly packed houses and felt sick. He was already aware of a sagging sensation beneath his legs. Chimney pots and church towers poked out of the gloom.

Above him the bird emitted a loud raucous screech and he glanced up to see that her blazing feathers had started to steam. The hail had lessened to a hard, steady rain, but the condensation was dampening her feathers, extinguishing her flame.

"Quick! Lighten our load!" yelled Mr. Hardy, as they continued to sink.

Cirrus immediately did as he was told, jettisoning whatever he could find from inside the basket. The bulk of St. Paul's was rushing nearer and he felt certain they were going to crash into the enormous columns of stone. But at the very last moment the man heaved on the ropes and steered the basket round the dome.

Pandora, beside him, was scouring the ground.

"Mr. Hardy!" she called out. "Madame Orrery's almost directly below us."

Cirrus peered down to see the silver carriage streaking along an adjacent passage.

"No matter," roared Mr. Hardy, fixing his sights on a nearby building. "We're almost there."

Cirrus turned to look where he was pointing.

Directly ahead of them was a vast structure with lofty windows and a tall metal pole that speared straight into the menacing clouds.

"What is that place?" he shouted over the noise of the driving rain.

"Mr. Sidereal's observatory," answered Pandora, handing him the spyglass. "Where your friend has gone."

Bottle Top!

Cirrus wiped the moisture from his face and pressed the lens to his eye. Instantly, his vision swooped across the surrounding rooftops. Through one of the many windows of the observatory he could see a small, hunched figure seated in a chair on wheels. Mr. Sidereal. Flickering jets of flame illuminated the walls around him.

A sudden movement caught his eye. Bottle Top had entered the room. Cirrus could barely breathe. A fist of anger had seized him by the throat.

"What is it?" asked Pandora.

"It's Bottle Top," he answered. "He's in there now."

Heart thumping, he watched as Bottle Top walked up to Mr. Sidereal and presented him with something from round his neck. His sphere! Cirrus could see the man studying it and turning the object in his fingers. And then, very slowly, a faint bluish white vapor leaked out, filling the chamber with a soft, swirling light.

"We're too late!" bellowed Mr. Hardy. "He's opened the sphere!"

Just then the balloon lurched to one side. Pandora grabbed Cirrus by the arm. "Look!" she said.

A maelstrom of sucking, spinning cloud had formed almost directly over the observatory, and the wind was hurling dust and grit into the air. The sky flickered with silver spears of light. Before Cirrus knew what was happening, several bolts of lightning had forked down and struck the long metal pole housing Mr. Sidereal's Scioptric Eye.

It was over in an instant.

A brief stab of light, a violent blast of air, followed by the brittle sound of exploding glass . . .

Cirrus had no time to think. He ducked down beside Pandora and clung to the sides of the basket as the force of the detonation catapulted them toward the clouds.

The wind shrilled through the ropes and tore at the sail, which it threatened to twist inside out, as they climbed a steep mountain of air. The blood spun dizzily in his head, and Cirrus had to clench his teeth to keep from calling out in fear. He was dimly aware of the girl crouched beside him, gasping for breath, and Alerion shrieking above them, scrabbling at her perch. Mr. Hardy, meanwhile, was doing everything in his power to maintain control of the shaking, shuddering craft.

Cirrus clamped his eyes shut, certain the assault would never end. But then, with a slight wobble, the vessel began to sink once more toward the ground. With a huge sigh of relief, he relaxed his hold of the basket and peered over the edge.

An angelic blue-and-white light was spreading rapidly over the city. It looked just like the heavenly substance that had radiated from his sphere the evening before, but on a far greater scale. It swept back and forth across the sky in diaphanous waves.

He gazed at it in wonder, lost for words.

Somehow the miraculous tide of light had washed the storm away. The rain had stopped and the thunder that still rumbled was faint and far away. Everything was calm, peaceful and still.

And then an anguished cry reached him from the ground.

The silver carriage had screeched to a halt outside the observatory and a woman in a long flowing gown had leapt out.

Her head was turned toward the sky and her features were contorted in a mask of rage. Cirrus, looking through the spyglass, recognized her as the woman who had hunted for him the other night at the hospital.

Beside him, Pandora had gone pale. "Madame Orrery," she said.

"Why is she so upset?"

"Because she wanted the Breath of God all for herself," said Pandora. "And now, I think, it's gone for good."

"The Breath of God?" asked Cirrus, staring again at the drifts of light.

"Aye," said Mr. Hardy. "It's what your father discovered at the edge of the world. The lightning that struck the observatory must have released it from the sphere."

Cirrus suddenly noticed the scene of devastation below him and went cold. The observatory had been destroyed, its windows shattered, its roof blown away.

"Bottle Top!" he cried.

Mr. Hardy very lightly laid a hand on the boy's shoulder. "I doubt he will have survived, son," he said.

Cirrus shook him off. He was trembling all over. "No!" he shouted. "Take me down! I need to find my friend!"

Pandora had turned away; there were tears in her eyes.

Mr. Hardy looked at the boy gravely and then, with a slight nod of his head, shifted his weight in the basket and steered them toward the ground.

The descent was infuriatingly slow. There was no wind to guide them and the vapor swirling above them cast a cold, crystal light. Cirrus kept his eyes on the rooftop, searching for his friend, but there was no sign of movement within the observatory's ruined shell.

He jumped down from the basket as soon as it came to a rest beside the remains of a shattered window. There was no need for an anchor; the air was perfectly still.

He entered what was left of the observatory and made his way through the debris, his footsteps crunching on the broken glass. Dust floated in the air and acrid twists of smoke curled from the ground. Tears pricked his eyes.

He found Mr. Sidereal first. The man was lying in the center of the room, not far from his chair, the remnants of the sphere still clutched in his hand. The last of its light had evaporated away. It was no good to anyone now.

Cirrus bent down and picked it up, twisting the halves together so that they formed a whole. The sphere felt strangely hollow. He draped it round his neck and then shakily continued his search for Bottle Top.

Finally, he spotted a thin white leg protruding from a bolt of black cloth, a heavy curtain that had fallen to the ground. Quietly, he crouched over it and took a deep breath. Then he pulled it back.

A sob rushed into his throat.

There, beneath, lay the body of his friend. Bottle Top, his wig singed by fire, his fine new clothes ragged and torn, his right arm twisted under him. His head was turned toward the sky, but his eyes were vacant and dull.

Cirrus stared for a moment and then a low, guttural moan

welled up inside him. It burst from his lungs and he rocked back and forth, cradling the lifeless form of his friend to his chest.

Pandora and Mr. Hardy stood a little way off, but did not come any closer. They left him to grieve on his own.

At last, Mr. Hardy put his arm round Pandora and led her gently away. "Come, let's see to the moon-sail," he said.

Eventually, Cirrus stumbled to his feet. His insides felt twisted and torn, just like the wreckage around him, and his eyes were brittle and sore. He could see Pandora and Mr. Hardy sitting by the edge of the rooftop and went over to join them.

Alerion fluttered down from a nearby perch and settled on the parapet beside him. She ruffled her wings and Cirrus could feel her hot fiery feathers drying the tears on his skin.

Below them the city was deserted. Even Madame Orrery, it seemed, had given up hope and driven away.

Cirrus looked at the light still sparkling and shimmering above them. It was fainter now, fading gradually.

"My father," he said softly, touching his sphere. "Who was he?"

Mr. Hardy smiled sadly and stared into the distance. "James Flux was my friend. We were foundlings together and went to sea. We were virtually inseparable."

Cirrus thought again of Bottle Top and the dreams they had shared. "What happened to him?" he asked, fighting to control his voice. "Why did he leave me?"

The man regarded him for a moment. "He had no choice," he said at last. "Your mother died giving birth to you. He took you to the safest place he knew: the Foundling Hospital." The ghost of a smile returned to his lips. "He always meant to take you back. He would have been proud to see you now."

Cirrus felt a flicker inside him, but Mr. Hardy was rising to his feet and dusting off his breeches. "Come, I'll tell you more about him when we get back to the hospital," he said.

"The hospital?" said Cirrus.

He glanced at the girl. Judging from the wilted expression on her face, she shared his sentiments. He wasn't certain where he belonged, but he did not feel ready yet to return to the hospital.

"Aye," said Mr. Hardy. "The Governor will be mighty worried about you. Not to mention Mrs. Kickshaw . . ."

"Can't you take us with you?" asked Pandora, her eager eyes aflame. "To the other side of the world?"

The man laughed uneasily, but shook his head. "What would I do with you, child?" he said. His voice, however, was tinged with regret. "I haven't got no home of my own, either."

"You could teach at the hospital," said Cirrus, voicing a sudden thought aloud. He glanced at the man's naval jacket and recalled how he had sailed them through the storm. "You could teach seamanship, perhaps."

"Moon-sailing!" said Pandora.

Mr. Hardy chuckled. "Now where would be the sense in that?" he asked, but the suggestion seemed to linger in his

280

mind. "I'll discuss it with the Governor," he said as he led them back toward the basket.

Cirrus, however, glanced at the figure of Bottle Top behind them. "What about my friend?" he asked. "We can't just leave him here."

"Aye," said Mr. Hardy. "We'll take him with us. There's a plot at the back of the hospital. We'll give him a proper burial."

The girl suddenly went pale and turned away. Cirrus looked at her, uncertain what to do. "Are you all right?" he asked her gently.

She wiped a tear from her eye. "I was just thinking of someone," she said, a slight tremor in her voice. "He's buried there, too."

Cirrus stared at the shards of broken glass on the ground, but did not reply. He waited for a moment and then reached out tentatively to take her hand.

"Come, let's go back," he said.

Her face warmed into a smile, but she shook her head. "No, not yet," she said. "There's something else I must do." She gazed into the distance, in the direction of Madame Orrery's departed carriage. "Something I must get."

❧ 23 ❧

H·O·P·E

Pandora eased herself onto the clothes chest below the window and jumped down, careful to avoid the glass that sprinkled the floor. She looked back and saw Mr. Hardy flying the moon-sail over the church tower opposite, preparing to tether the basket to the statue of St. George. Only a few days before, he had rescued her from this bedroom prison; now, in the middle of the night, she was sneaking back in.

"Be quick," he had warned her. "We'll be waiting outside if anything goes wrong."

She had nodded and given a small smile. The boy had offered to come with her, but she needed to do this on her own. Back on the observatory rooftop, there had been an ache in her heart. She could not help thinking of her twin brother, buried at the hospital, and longed once more to feel her mother's well-worn piece of fabric in her hands.

Her fingers traced the familiar letters in the air: H-O-P-E.

It was then she realized what she must do.

Taking a quick look around, she crossed the bedroom floor and passed through the open door into the dark, deserted corridor. Below her the house was quiet. It would be several hours, she knew, before Mr. Sorrel awoke.

Stepping lightly, she moved along the passage and felt her way down the stairs.

The kitchen, when she got there, was dark and cold. Ashes filled the grate. She lit a candle using the tinderbox Mr. Sorrel kept by the hearth and shaded the flame with her hand. Shaking a little, she grabbed a ring of keys from its hook beside the door and followed the trembling path of light back through the house to the hall.

The curtains to the Crisis Room were open and she could just make out the Mesmerism Tub within, sitting in a pool of darkness, surrounded by a ring of empty chairs. She thought briefly of the patients she had seen sprawled on the floor, purged of their painful memories, and quickly turned up the stairs.

She had never set foot inside Madame Orrery's private apartment before and now that she was on the threshold she nearly lost her nerve. She listened closely and then, taking a deep breath, inserted the key in the lock and twisted it round.

The door inched open and she stepped in.

She gasped. A figure was watching her from an adjacent doorway, just visible in the gloom. A pale, headless figure, dressed in one of Madame Orrery's silver gowns. Pandora caught her breath. It was a dummy, nothing else. The woman's bedchamber must lie beyond.

Clutching her candle, Pandora stepped nervously around the room, hunting for a sign of her mother's cloth. Where would the woman keep it? Fearfully, she checked the hearth, but there was no indication that it had been burned.

She moved quietly toward the adjoining door.

In the next room she found a large four-poster bed, surrounded by damask curtains, all of which had been pulled back. Madame Orrery lay within, her hair draped across the pillow in a messy gossamer web. The shutters were open and, through the dark panes of glass, Pandora could see wisps of light shimmering back and forth—the Breath of God still just visible in the sky. Madame Orrery's face was turned toward it, although Pandora could not tell from here whether she was awake.

She crept closer, as soft as a moth, anxious for the slightest movement.

Shadows crawled across the woman's face, but her eyes were closed and there were faint flutters beneath the lids. Pandora was surprised by how old and tired Madame Orrery looked.

She froze.

Something shimmered on the pillow, next to Madame Orrery's head. It was the silver timepiece, ticking ever so quietly in the dark. Just the sight of it sent a shudder down her neck and Pandora thought of turning back, terrified the woman might roll over and fix her with one of her chilling looks.

And then she noticed the scrap of fabric, clutched like a petal, in the woman's hand. She tiptoed toward it, her heart in her throat.

The floorboard creaked behind her and Pandora jumped. She spun round. Mr. Sorrel was watching her from the doorway.

For a moment she feared he was going to call out and wake Madame Orrery, but then his eyes passed from Pandora's frightened face to the scrap of fabric in his mistress's hand. He gave her an encouraging nod.

With the deftest of movements, Pandora plucked it from the sleeping woman's grasp and followed Mr. Sorrel back into the adjoining room.

"I did not expect to see you again, my child," he said, once they were safely out of earshot. He gazed thoughtfully at the piece of fabric in her hand. "*Hope*," he said, and gave a little smile. "A quality I should have thought you already possessed in abundance."

Pandora was conscious of the silver timepiece ticking in the darkness behind her and was tempted to run back and snatch it, so that Madame Orrery could never think of mesmerizing anyone again, but then she remembered how Mr. Sorrel seemed genuinely to believe in its power to cure people of their pasts. Once again she wondered how he had come to serve Madame Orrery.

"What will you do?" she asked at last. "The sphere

belonging to Cirrus Flux has been destroyed. Madame Orrery cannot have it."

Mr. Sorrel was silent for a moment. "I shall continue to serve Madame Orrery as I always have done," he said simply, and then paused, seeming to reconsider. "I am afraid, Pandora, that I am not able to remember much of my past, but I am certain that Madame Orrery must have saved me from a dire situation." He seemed to read the doubtful expression on her face, for he stopped. "Please, Pandora, you must not judge her so harshly. She has overcome much hardship and suffering in her life. Yet while she can ease the pain of others, she has never been able to heal herself."

He regarded her thoughtfully. "And you, Pandora," he said. "Where will you go?"

Pandora thought suddenly of Cirrus and Mr. Hardy waiting for her on the church tower opposite and her spirits lifted.

"I am going where I belong," she said with a smile. And, clutching her mother's keepsake, she moved toward the door.

ACKNOWLEDGMENTS

When I started this book I knew very little about the eighteenth century, a period of great exploration, scientific discovery and philosophical debate, commonly known in Britain as the Age of Enlightenment. Among the many books that have helped me to conjure up a picture of this fascinating world are: Richard D. Altick's *The Shows of London* (1978), which features an illustration of Mr. Sidereal's chair and a description of the Holophusikon, the model for Mr. Leechcraft's Hall of Wonders; Emily Cockayne's *Hubbub: Filth, Noise & Stench in England 1600–1770* (2007), which brings the sights, smells and sounds of Georgian society to life; Robert Darnton's *Mesmerism and the End of the Enlightenment in France* (1968), which taught Madame Orrery everything she knows; Patricia Fara's *An Entertainment for Angels* (2002), which sheds light on the truly shocking treatment of Hanging Boys; Francis Grose's *A Classical Dictionary of the Vulgar Tongue* (1785), which taught me how to curse, eighteenth-century style; Richard Hamblyn's *The Invention of Clouds* (2001), which opened my eyes to the strange weather of 1783 and the appearance of the first hot-air balloons; Samuel Johnson's *Dictionary* (1755), which informed me that "Cirrus Flux" is not only an unlikely name for a boy in the eighteenth century, but also a highly unflattering one ("flux" meant "diarrhoea" at the time); Ruth McClure's *Coram's Children: The London Foundling Hospital in the Eighteenth Century* (1981), which depicts life in the Foundling Hospital far more accurately than I do; and Liza Picard's *Dr. Johnson's London* (2001), which took me on a fabulous ramble through the streets of London.

My learning wasn't confined to books. I'm also indebted to Jaco Groot and Elsbeth Louis of Uitgeverij De Harmonie, as well as the helpful staff of the Teylers Museum in Haarlem, for showing me Martinus van Marum's electrostatic machine (which Mr. Leechcraft stole and used for his own purposes in the Hall of Wonders); "The Proceedings of the Old Bailey" online, which is an amazingly rich source of information; and the Foundling Museum in London, where some of the original children's tokens are on display. I should also like to thank my family and friends for their support—and the many readers who have written to me with words of encouragement. I couldn't have finished this book without them.